JESSICA BECK

THE DONUT MYSTERIES, BOOK 28

MIXED MALICE

The First Time Ever Published!

The 28th Donut Mystery.

Jessica Beck is the *New York Times* Bestselling Author of the Donut Mysteries, the Classic Diner Mysteries, the Ghost Cat Cozy Mysteries, and the Cast Iron Cooking Mysteries.

To P, forever and always,
for all the years, all the laughs, and all the love!

During the remodeling of Donut Hearts after a big ice storm damaged the place, contractor Snappy Mack is found murdered inside the shop, and Suzanne and Jake must find the killer before he strikes again. As they search through the remnants of the contractor's life, they soon realize that too many folks had a reason to want to see Snappy dead, and sorting it all out is going to be no easy task.

CHAPTER 1

"**H**ELLO? IS ANYONE HERE?" I asked tentatively as I peered into the darkness and put one foot inside Donut Hearts, my heart pounding in my ears.

It was nearly pitch black inside my donut shop, which really wasn't that surprising, given the hour. At three o'clock in the morning, I hadn't been expecting anyone else to be there, since Emma didn't come in until four, so I usually had the place to myself at that time of morning.

So why was the front door standing ajar?

Was it possible that Snappy Mack, my new contractor, had left the shop unlocked after he'd finished working for the evening? We were trying to fit two full-time schedules into a static twenty-four-hour day, and I wasn't at all sure how it was going to work. I was there from three to a little after eleven every morning, while Snappy took over at one p.m. and worked until who knew when. Had he left to get new materials to repair the shop and not bothered to come back? Snappy was the bottom of the barrel for me, but at least my mother had been able to find *someone* to fix the place up after a large oak tree had smashed into Donut Hearts in the middle of the worst ice storm we'd had for as long as I could remember. I'd been expecting Snappy to get started on the job well before Christmas, but here it was the second day of a brand-new year, and I was beginning to wonder if it was ever going to get finished. My contractor was still working on the demolition stage, and I wasn't sure I'd

1

ever actually see real progress on restoring my donut shop to a shadow of its former glory.

"Snappy?" I called out as I stepped all the way inside. "Did you fall asleep again?" It pained me to learn that our police chief, Stephen Grant, had discovered Snappy dozing off instead of working just the day before. "If you nodded off, it's time to wake up. Rise and shine, sleepyhead," I called out as I flipped on the lights.

In a split second, it was clear that Snappy would never be getting up again.

Someone had seen to that.

The construction worker was lying facedown in the middle of the donut shop's concrete floor with the handle of a screwdriver poking out of his back.

At least the handle was the only part that I could see.

I took a few quick photos with my phone out of habit more than anything else, then I stepped back outside quickly and called the police chief as my foot brushed against a faded old newspaper on the floor with traces of blood on it.

It appeared that murder had just paid another visit to my not-so-quiet little town of April Springs, North Carolina.

After I called Chief Grant and told him what had happened to poor Snappy, my husband was the next name on my list. I didn't call Jake just because I needed his support in such a trying time, though that was true enough. The fact of the matter was that he also happened to be a retired state police inspector and the former interim police chief for our town before he'd handed the duties over to our current chief law enforcement officer, Stephen Grant.

"Jake, it's Suzanne," I said, fighting to catch my breath and calm my rapidly beating heart.

"Hey, Suzanne. What's up?" I knew for a fact that he'd been sleeping when I'd left him ten minutes earlier, so how on earth did he sound so alert now?

"I didn't wake you, did I?" I asked him, a completely ridiculous question to ask any sane person at three o'clock in the morning.

"I'm fine. Did you forget your keys?"

"I wish it were something that mundane," I told him. "I just found Snappy Mack dead in the middle of the donut shop."

"What happened? Did he have a heart attack?" Jake asked me, a legitimate question since Snappy had a spare tire around his waist big enough for a tractor-trailer.

"Not unless he died of fright just before someone stabbed him in the back with a screwdriver," I replied.

"Are you still inside?" he asked, his voice now coming through loudly.

"No, I stepped outside to call Chief Grant, and then I wanted to call you and bring you up to speed on what happened here," I said.

"Get away from the donut shop. Run! I mean right now!" His voice was strong and commanding, very hard to ignore.

"Jake, whoever killed my contractor didn't hang around to watch me make donuts," I explained.

"Do as I say, please?" he asked. The concern was thick in his voice.

I wasn't a big fan of taking orders from anyone, even my husband, but I knew that his reaction was out of love. "Fine. I'm leaving," I said, not running but walking toward my Jeep, not that it would have offered me a great deal of protection if the killer had still been hanging around. It was a ragtop, and it would take something substantially less than a knife to get to me.

"Why aren't you running away?" Jake asked me as he approached less than a minute later.

"I guess I just ran out of steam," I explained.

My husband raised one eyebrow, showing me that he didn't believe one word of my excuse, as he started for the door. His service weapon was in his hand, but I noticed that he hadn't even stopped to put on his shoes before he'd come to me, even though it was barely kissing thirty degrees out.

"Not to put too fine a point on things, but shouldn't you wait for the police?" I asked him before he could go inside.

"I'll do just fine until they show," Jake said. As he approached the front door, Chief Grant drove up and slammed his squad car to a vibrating halt within three inches of my Jeep.

"Hang on, Jake. I'm going in with you," the chief said as he leapt from his car.

Jake merely nodded, and a moment later, the two men went inside, both their weapons drawn.

It suddenly occurred to me that if the killer *was* still hanging around, maybe he was lurking in the bushes outside where I was, waiting for the men with guns to go away.

If that ended up turning out to be the case, I really had better be ready to run.

With every passing second they were gone, I kept glancing back and forth from the shop to the darkened park, until finally I heard Jake call out to me from the door, "It's all clear, Suzanne. No one's here."

"Except Snappy, you mean," I said, still seeing the image of the man's dead body in my mind. It was an image I knew I was going to have a hard time wiping from my memory, but I was going to do my best nonetheless.

"I know you aren't going to be happy with me, but I'm afraid I'm going to have to shut Donut Hearts down this morning,"

Chief Grant said. "We need to secure the crime scene and analyze the evidence before any of it gets lost in the shuffle."

"I understand completely," I said as I started to brush past him and head inside.

"Whoa. Where exactly do you think you're going?" he asked me, barring my way.

"I need to at least make a sign for my customers," I explained.

"I think they'll get the message that you're not open for business when they see the crime scene tape and all of the squad cars out front," Chief Grant said. Then he turned to Jake and added, "Thanks for the backup."

"I should be thanking you for letting me tag along," he said. "Suzanne, how about a ride home? My feet are freezing."

"That's what you get for running out of the house barefoot in January," I told him as he got into the passenger seat of my Jeep.

"You should feel lucky I took the time to put on my pants," he said with a wry grin as he buckled his seatbelt.

"I'm not sure who would have seen the show if you hadn't, given this time of night." I let out a deep breath, and then I added, "I wasn't Snappy's biggest fan, but who would want to kill the man, especially in my donut shop? It just doesn't make sense."

"I have no idea, but I have a feeling we're going to try to find out, aren't we?" Jake asked as he stared at me. "Since Grace is out of town for a sales meeting, could you use a second-in-command?"

"You know I could," I said. "As long as you're content with that and don't try to lead my investigation for me."

"No worries on that count. I won't make that mistake again," he said with a smile. "Should we get started now, or do you want to wait until *after* the sun comes up?"

"Well, I doubt anyone is going to want to talk to us at this hour," I said, and then I suddenly remembered that Emma didn't know what had happened at Donut Hearts. "I can't believe I forgot. I need to call Emma and tell her what happened," I said to Jake as I pulled into our driveway. It was just a three-minute commute, merely one of the many things I loved about my job.

"I'll be inside warming up," he said. "Why don't you chat with her as you come in with me?"

"Jake, we're in front of our own cottage. I'm sure that I'll be perfectly safe here."

"Just to be certain, do it my way, would you?" he asked me.

"I suppose I could," I said as I dialed Emma's number and started to follow my husband inside. My assistant picked up on the tenth ring, and at least she had the decency to sound as though I'd woken her.

"Someone killed Snappy Mack inside Donut Hearts," I told her. "We're taking today off."

"Would it be okay with you if I woke my dad and told him?" Emma asked me, abiding by our strict rules of keeping her father's newspaper and our donut shop completely separate. Her dad, Ray Blake, owned and ran the *April Springs Sentinel*, the town's lone news-reporting medium, and there had been several instances in the past when our paths had crossed with unpleasant results.

"I don't see why not," I said. After all, the entire town would know about Snappy's murder by morning anyway, so why not give Ray a break and let him have the scoop?

"Thanks. You're the best, boss."

"So I've been told," I said, but I was talking to dead air. Emma had already hung up.

"So, what should we do now?" I asked Jake. "It's too early to start knocking on doors asking questions about Snappy."

"We could always just stay inside and brainstorm for a while," my husband said.

"Is that code for taking a nap?" I asked him with the hint of a smile. There wasn't much to be happy about at the moment, but having Jake by my side was at least something. I hadn't wanted to linger at the donut shop. The image of Snappy being carted off in a body bag was not something I needed to see. I'd deal with the cleanup later, which reminded me that I had to find a new contractor as soon as possible. Was that callous, coming so soon after finding the last one's body? Maybe, but I had to be pragmatic about it, too. "Jake, am I some kind of monster?"

"Why would you ask me that?" he asked as he added a few logs to the fire to bring the fading flames back to life. "Of course not."

"One of the things I just thought about was that I was going to have to find a new contractor. Care to rethink your previous answer now?"

"Not even a little bit," he said. "The work still needs to get finished. Just not today."

"How long do you think the chief will keep my shop closed down?" I asked him as we settled onto the couch.

"The best answer I have is as long as it takes," Jake said.

"Wow, what an illuminating response," I said in a dry tone.

"That's not how I meant it, but it's tough knowing something like that. If I had to guess, I'd say Donut Hearts will be yours again by noon, but like I said, that's just a guess."

"Then it won't do me any good today," I said. I'd held out the slimmest of hopes that I'd get Donut Hearts back in time to at least knock out some cake donuts for my customers. It wasn't about the money; I didn't care if I had to give them away. I just wanted to wash the bad old memories of what had just happened there with some new, happier images.

Evidently it would have to wait until the next day, though.

"I can't believe Snappy was murdered in my shop," I said as I watched the flames start in on the fresh logs. "As far as I'm concerned, donut shops should be the happiest places on earth."

"I think someone else already beat you to that slogan," Jake said with a smile.

"If you can get donuts there too, then I agree," I replied. Jake chuckled, and I added, "It may not make sense to the rest of the world, but it makes perfect sense to me, based on my own internal logic." After staring at the flames for a minute, I asked my husband, "Do you happen to know anything about Snappy Mack?"

"Just what I've learned since the renovation got started," Jake answered. My husband had spent an hour or two at the donut shop after hours the day before, so it wouldn't have surprised me to discover that he knew my contractor quite a bit better than I did.

"Are there any suspects in your mind, then?"

"Let's see. Snappy's been having problems with his girlfriend lately, and his business partner is breathing down his neck about increasing his monthly salary from the business. Then there's Snappy's son, a bad seed if ever there was one, according to the contractor, at least."

"I didn't even know Snappy *had* a son. What's his name, Zippy?"

"No, it's Sanderson Wentworth Mack the Fourth," Jake said.

"If that were my name, I might have people call me 'Snappy' too," I said. "How did you find out so much about the man's life in such a short amount of time? I'm not criticizing you. It's amazing."

"Suzanne, half the work I did as a cop was interviewing suspects and figuring out if they were telling me the truth or not. I find myself asking leading questions of just about everybody I meet these days. For instance, did you know that your flour supplier is thinking about getting engaged?"

"Melissa? I didn't even realize she was dating anyone steady."

"She's not," Jake said with a grin. "She came by when I was

chatting with Snappy, and we started talking outside. It appears Melissa is envious of you and what we have together."

"Well, she can't have you," I said with a grin. "You're taken."

"I don't think she was implying that I should leave you for her. She was just lamenting the fact that there weren't any good men left."

"What did you say to that?"

"I gave her an old friend's phone number," Jake reluctantly admitted, clearly embarrassed about being caught matchmaking. "In my defense, the last time I spoke with Terry Hanlan, he said nearly the exact same thing to me, that he was getting frustrated by the absence of a good woman in his life. It just seemed like the right thing to do, putting them in touch with each other."

"So, matchmaking runs in the family," I said, doing my best not to gloat. Jake had teased me in the past about my proclivity to set people up, and here he was doing it himself now.

"I won't concede the validity of your point," he said. "Now, can we please get back to Snappy Mack and who might have wanted to kill him?"

"Sure thing," I said, knowing that, though I was willing to table this discussion for the moment, we would be talking about it again, and soon. "You didn't happen to catch any of those names besides his son, did you? Ordinarily I'd say that the idea of a son killing his own father was too sad to even contemplate, but he did name him Sanderson, so I'm not so sure."

"Lots of men have family names they are burdened with," Jake said. "It's not motive enough for murder, Suzanne."

"I was just teasing. All I'm saying is that if there was animosity between the two men, he needs to go on our list."

"Agreed," Jake said. "The partner's name should be easy enough to find out, and as for the girlfriend, I keep thinking it belongs to a country."

"Something like America?" I asked him with a hint of laughter in my voice.

"Strike that. Not a country, a city. Let's see. Atlanta? No. Charlotte? I don't think so. Cheyenne? No, Madison. That's it, I'm certain!"

"Good. It sounds as though we've already made some real progress," I said, and then I glanced at the clock on my phone. It was just a few minutes past four a.m. "Too bad that it's still too early to start checking on these folks."

"You know, a little nap wouldn't hurt while we wait for a more reasonable hour," Jake said. "The fire is warm, and it may be late for you, but I'm still on my own time schedule. What do you think about taking a little rest before we get started?"

"Actually, it sounds delightful to me," I said as I snuggled a little closer to my husband. "Wake me if you get up first."

His laughter served to soothe my troubled spirit. "I'm not entirely sure that's even possible," he said. "Good night. Again."

"Good night," I said.

I was afraid that I might have trouble drifting off to sleep, but a combination of the warm fire, my husband beside me, and the shock of finding my contractor's body all served to knock me out almost immediately, and I was asleep before I knew it.

CHAPTER 2

"Wow, I can't believe I'm getting a full breakfast this morning," Jake said as I served him eggs, bacon, toast, and hash browns the moment he took his place at the table. I hadn't planned on putting out such a varied spread, but I'd awoken well before I should have, and besides, I was used to being busy early in the morning. He jabbed his fork at me as he asked, "Suzanne, are you sure you don't want anything?"

"Like I told you earlier, I already ate," I said with a grin. I'd been planning to wait so I could eat with him, but my hunger pains hadn't allowed it. "Well, just to keep you company, I might have a nibble or two while you eat," I added as I took a piece of bacon and ate it. It was made from turkey and still quite good, but I missed real pork bacon sometimes. We had adopted some better eating habits, at least while we were at home, since Jake's last doctor's checkup. He'd been told that some of his cholesterol numbers were high, and I was doing my best to help them get back into acceptable ranges if it killed us both.

"You almost can't tell it's not real," Jake said with a smile of his own as he bit into another piece.

"Hey, at least it's not made out of wheat germ paste or something like that," I said.

"Is that actually a thing?"

My husband looked so horrified by the prospect that I had

to laugh. "I don't know, but don't worry. I won't feed you any, even if it is."

Jake finished eating, and I was getting started on clearing the dishes when the doorbell rang. It was still before seven a.m., and though Jake and I were both used to being up by then, it was still odd having any visitors at that hour.

"I'll go see who it is," Jake said as he started to stand.

"Not without me, you won't," I answered, leaving everything right where it was sitting so I could join him.

"Momma, what a nice surprise," I said as I opened the door to find my petite mother, alone, standing on the front porch. "You know you don't have to actually ring the bell. Feel free to just walk on in. After all, you gave me this place, remember?"

"That's right, and as such, that means that it's not mine anymore," Momma replied as she stepped in and kissed Jake's cheek. I got one as well before she took in a deep breath as she pulled her jacket off. "Am I interrupting breakfast?"

"No, ma'am, we were just finishing up. I made plenty, though, if you'd like a plate."

"Thank you, but I start my days most mornings with yogurt and fruit."

"I'm so sorry," Jake told her with a smile.

"Don't be," she answered with a chuckle. "It suits me."

"Momma, not that I don't love seeing you, but this *is* early even for you." And then I got it. "You heard about Snappy, didn't you?"

"What an unfortunate name for a grown man," she said with a hint of sadness in her voice. "It's all over town. Somehow I feel responsible for what happened in your shop this morning."

"You shouldn't, Dot. Not unless you were the one wielding the screwdriver, that is," Jake replied.

She shuddered at the thought. "No, but I'm the one who brought him to town to work at Donut Hearts. If I hadn't interfered, he wouldn't have been there this morning or last night. Whenever it happened."

"Do you honestly think that his murder was directly related to the donut shop?" I asked her, surprised by the very thought of it.

"What? No! Of course not! I believe no such thing."

"Okay," I said, trying to calm her down again. "I didn't mean to imply something that wasn't true. It just sounded as though that was how you felt."

"Let me assure you, I don't. Still, it couldn't have been pleasant for you to stumble into your shop first thing in the morning and find the poor man's body waiting for you."

"It wasn't," I said, not really wanting to get into it again, at least not with Momma. I knew I'd be asked about finding Snappy a hundred times before the sun set again, but one of them shouldn't be from my own mother. "Jake and I are going to find out who killed him," I said matter-of-factly, getting it out of the way before she could say anything to the contrary to try to dissuade us.

"Hang on a second, Suzanne," my husband said. "I'm not exactly sure we can say that."

"Have you changed your mind, Jake? Don't you want to investigate with me?" It surprised me that he might be getting cold feet.

"Not on your life. If you're in, then so am I. What I was trying to say was that we're going to do our best to add to the police investigation, but I have no delusions that we're going to be naming a killer within forty-eight hours or anything like that."

"You don't? Really? That's funny. I expect to do it every time," I answered truthfully. "It might not always work out that way, but there's no reason not to believe that it might. Jake, we need to get something clear up front. Are you absolutely certain that you want to do this with me?"

"Perhaps I should have called first," Momma said as she reached for her jacket.

We both looked at her and shook our heads in perfect unison. "No, you shouldn't have. Stay right where you are."

Jake and I grinned at each other for a moment before he said, "I was by no means expressing anything less than my full confidence in our abilities and our desire to solve this murder. There, is that better?"

"Much," I said as I kissed him quickly. After that, I turned to Momma and asked, "Since you're here, what can you tell us about Snappy, since you're the one who found him?"

"What do you know so far?" she asked.

"Jake spoke with him the other day," I explained, "and during the course of their conversation, he found out that there are at least three people in Maple Hollow who might have a reason to do it: his girlfriend, a young woman named Madison, his business partner, a fellow named Hank, and the man's own son, Sanderson Mack."

"My, were you investigating his life even then, before the murder?" Momma asked, clearly impressed by what Jake had managed to collect without even meaning to.

"If you knew the man at all, I don't have to tell you that Snappy liked to talk about himself," Jake told my mother. It was as humble an answer as he could give, but it didn't surprise me. I'd found over the years that the better someone was at doing something, the less they felt the need to brag about their abilities to others.

"I knew that he liked to talk, but I never knew all of that. The truth of the matter is that he only did one minor job for me last month on a store I own in Maple Hollow. He seemed to do a good job, and he was the only one I could get to come to April Springs on short notice to fix Donut Hearts."

"I have to admit that it surprised me when you recommended

a contractor from Maple Hollow that I'd never heard of," I said. "Whatever happened to Hank Caldwell?" Hank had done some work for us on my great aunt Jean's house after her murder. Momma and I had both been skating around mentioning her again. The memory of our loss was still pretty strong in each of us.

"From what I understand, he retired and moved to Florida," Momma said.

"Did his assistant carry on the business?" I asked. "What was his name, Craig?"

"Close. It's Greg; Greg Raymond. He's taken over, but he was tied up, along with most of my other contacts in the building trades," Momma explained. "I believe he's going to run for Hank's seat on the city council soon."

"How do you happen to know so much about that little town? I've only been back a few times since Aunt Jean died."

"As I said before, I have some business interests there," she said wistfully. "I actually went by her old house the other day. They've butchered the trees and the shrubs on the property. Jean would have been horrified."

"I'm sorry to hear that," I said, realizing just how painful the memory was for my mother.

"About the greenery? Don't be. They own it now; it is theirs to do with as they wish," Momma said as she wiped away an errant tear. "Now, is there anything I can do to facilitate your investigation?"

"Right now we're just gathering information," Jake explained, "but we might need your contacts in Maple Hollow if you're really not opposed to helping us with this."

"I'd be delighted to aid you in any manner I can. Remember, I'm never more than a telephone call away," she said, and then Momma grabbed her coat and started for the door. "I'm equally certain that offer goes for my husband as well. I'm sure Phillip would love to be included if the circumstances allow it."

"And you?" I asked her. "Do you want to get involved in the case as *more* than a silent partner?" Momma had helped me solve Aunt Jean's murder, but she hadn't done much in the supporting role since.

"No, I'll gladly leave that to all of you," she said. "Too many cooks and all of that, you know." Momma started for the door, but then she hesitated before stopping and pulling a business card from her pocket. "That reminds me. I've got another contractor lined up for you. His last name is Young; he's a little brusque, but he's available, he's good, and given what happened to your last contractor, this one's on me."

"I appreciate the recommendation, but I can't take anything else from you, Momma," I said, pushing the card back toward her.

"Suzanne, I have only one daughter. Please let me spoil you."

Jake stepped up and took the card. "Thanks. We appreciate that, Dot. We'll discuss the financial aspects of it after we hear from the insurance company."

It was a bold move on my husband's part, but I knew that he'd done it in the name of expediency, mainly because all three of us fully realized that I'd end up taking the card, and most likely her generous offer, in the long run.

Momma decided to quit while she was ahead. "Remember, call me if you need me. Phillip as well."

"We will. And thanks again," I said as I plucked the contractor's business card from Jake's hand and waved it in the air.

"Of course," she said.

After Momma was gone, Jake said gently, "I'm truly sorry about that. I knew I should stay out of it, and yet I walked right into something between your mother and you."

The look of contrition on his face was so sincere that I couldn't bring myself to be cross with him. "It's fine, as long as it doesn't become a habit," I said gently.

"No worries on that count," Jake replied. "Let's put the leftovers away and then head out for Maple Hollow. What do you say?"

"That sounds like a good plan to me, but I need to make one phone call first," I said as I took out my phone and dialed the number on the card. After all, I hated what had happened to Snappy Mack, but I still needed my donut shop returned to its former glory, and as far as I was concerned, the sooner he could get started, the better.

CHAPTER 3

"**W**HAT'S THE WORD?" JAKE ASKED me after I hung up the phone.

"Do you want the good news or the bad news first?" I asked my husband.

"Bad news. Always the bad news first."

"Why is that?"

"Well, I figure I can always use some good news after hearing the bad first," Jake answered with a slight smile.

"Mr. Young, or just plain Young, as he prefers to be called, can't get started for three more days," I said.

"That's not the worst news I've ever heard," my husband said, and then he quickly backtracked the moment he saw my dour expression. "I mean, in the scope of things like complete world destruction, and things like that."

"That's a pretty stout bar you've set there," I said.

"And the good news?"

"Once he gets started, he thinks he and his crew can finish the entire job in two days. That's a full restoration to all its former glory, and with a few new improvements inside, too. I think he's overstating his ability, but he seemed sure of his schedule."

"What are you going to change about Donut Hearts?" Jake asked me, clearly unsure about how he felt changing something that was so much a part of me.

"Well, for one thing, the floor never has been level in the dining area, so I'm going to take advantage of having the chunks patched and get that taken care of. Then it's going to be a different color. I've had enough plum to last me a lifetime."

"Any ideas on the new color the floor might be?"

"Not yet, but don't worry. I'll keep you posted," I said.

"While you were talking to your new contractor, I took a chance and called Chief Grant," Jake admitted. "I'm sorry I didn't wait for you to get off your call, but I figured I might as well touch base with the man while I had a minute."

"That makes sense," I said calmly.

My reaction, or lack of it, seemed to surprise my husband. "That's it? You really don't mind?"

"No, sir. I figure I'll save the things I really care about for what's important. Did he have any news for us?"

"Quite a bit, actually. He's already spoken with our suspects," Jake said. "The man is growing exponentially in his job skills."

"You sound surprised. Why wouldn't he be improving? After all, he's had a great teacher," I said, since Jake had taken the young police chief under his wing when he'd been the interim chief of police.

"There are things you can teach, and then there are things you just have to learn on your own," Jake said, deflecting my praise.

I wasn't about to argue the point with him. "Did he have any luck with our suspects?"

"Not so far. It doesn't help matters that he's conducting a joint investigation with the chief there. Kessler is a good man, but he's in over his head when it comes to murder." Jake had met the Maple Hollow police chief briefly after Momma and I had solved Aunt Jean's murder, and he was a better judge of the man's competence than I was.

"Is our chief going to be okay with us investigating in April Springs?" I asked.

"He told me that as long as we stay out of Kessler's way and keep touching base with him, we'll be fine. If it's all the same to you, I say we avoid Maple Hollow's chief of police and go about our business."

"Don't you have to check in with him or something when you go to his town?" I asked.

"Why would I have to do that? I'm not on the job anywhere anymore. As far as the world's concerned, I'm just another concerned citizen."

"With a long history in law enforcement," I corrected for him.

"We should be all right. Besides, Chief Grant already warned him that we'd be sniffing around at the edges of this case."

"I'm not sure interviewing the main suspects the day of the murder could be qualified as being at the edge of anything," I said.

"Maybe not," Jake said with a slight laugh, "but Chief Grant wants our opinions of all three of our suspects."

"He wants yours, maybe," I said. "I'm not so sure about mine."

"No, there you're wrong. He was most specific that he wanted to hear what you have to say as well. Suzanne, the police chief thinks a great deal of your insights."

"That's flattering," I said, not really knowing what else I could say to that.

"Let's not disappoint him, then, okay? What do you say?"

"Did the chief happen to mention when I could get my donut shop back?" I asked my husband. I knew he'd posed the question without even asking him if he'd covered that particular topic.

"One p.m., and not a minute sooner," Jake said with a hint of resignation.

I thought about it and wondered what could possibly take so long, but it was a battle I didn't want to fight. "Then let's use the time we have wisely and head to Maple Hollow right now."

From the way Jake had been watching me, he'd clearly been expecting an explosion. When I'd failed to deliver, he'd been more than a little surprised. "Suzanne, are you feeling okay? I know how you feel about Donut Hearts, and it can't be easy shutting it down for the day."

"I love the place. Now try to imagine how outraged I am that someone had the audacity to kill my contractor in it. We need to find this murderer, Jake, and we need to do it quickly."

"I'll do my best to do my part," he said. "The weather forecast is for sunny skies in the mid-thirties. We should take my truck."

Normally I liked to drive my Jeep, and Jake knew it, but he had a point. We wouldn't be needing my all-weather traction, and I knew that my husband liked to drive every now and then, too. "Sold."

"Why do I have the feeling that you're giving in way too easily on too many things today, Suzanne?"

"Are you implying that I'm not always this easy to get along with?" I asked him sweetly.

My dear husband was too smart to step into that particular trap. "Let's get going," he said, completely ignoring my question.

He was indeed a wise man, just one of the many reasons that I'd fallen in love with him.

As we pulled into Maple Hollow, I felt myself tearing up, remembering my late Aunt Jean. Jake must have noticed, because he put his hand gently on my knee as he asked, "Are you okay, Suzanne?"

"It's just that this place holds a lot of memories for me," I explained. "I'll be fine."

"We don't have to do this, you know."

"I appreciate the gesture, Jake, but Snappy was murdered in my shop. There is no way I'm *not* going to play my part in finding out who did it." I wiped the last of the tears away and did my best to smile brightly at my husband. "Now, where should we head first?"

"I was thinking we should speak with Hank Bloch, Snappy's business partner. I'm curious to see how closely Snappy's description of the man matches what we find."

"That sounds like a solid plan to me," I said.

"Do you think he'll actually be in the office the day his partner was found murdered?"

"If he's like most of the small business owners I've known in my life, he'll be there," I said. "He probably can't afford not to. If I didn't have Emma, how many days could I keep the donut shop closed before it became a problem?"

"I don't know. How many?"

"Let me put it this way. There's a reason Donut Hearts is open seven days a week, and it's not because we all don't have anything better to do," I said.

"I get it. Now, according to what Snappy told me the other day, their place should be somewhere around here." As Jake drove down a side street that was barely bigger than an alley, he said, "There it is."

The building looked as though it were in need of remodeling more than my donut shop was. Metal roofing on the two-story building seemed to flap in the breeze, the cinderblock walls were in bad need of a coat of paint, and the truck parked out front made Jake's old beater look like this year's model.

"It's not much to look at, is it?" I asked as Jake parked beside the truck.

"Don't kid yourself. A lot of tradesmen don't want to give the impression that they're prosperous."

"Well then, I'd say they're doing a good job of disguising it if that's the case," I said as we approached the front door. I'd started to knock when Jake reached for the handle. It opened to his touch, and he grinned at me as he walked in ahead of me.

A young man, husky and prematurely balding, was sitting at the desk, wading through massive stacks of paper. He looked surprised to see us when Jake cleared his throat.

"Sorry, folks," he said, "but we're not open for business today. There's been a death in the family."

"We know," I said. "I'm Suzanne Hart."

Before I could say anything else, he interrupted me. "The donut lady. Yeah, I hate to tell you this, but it looks like we're going to have to cancel that job. There's no way I'll ever be able to get to it in time without Snappy. I wish we could refund your down payment, but we're already into the job for more than you gave us."

"I'm not here to get my money back," I said, doing my best to keep my temper in check at the outlandish statement.

"If that's the truth, then you're the first one today who hasn't been."

"Are things going to be all that tough with Snappy gone?" Jake asked as he looked at the stack of papers.

"You might say that," Bloch said with a sigh. "I'm sorry to say that my partner was the bookkeeper of the two of us, but that's not saying much. We were both better builders than accountants. The truth of the matter is that I don't think I'm going to keep going now that he's gone."

"Surely you need the business now more than ever, though," I said.

Bloch leaned back and put his hands behind his head. "Who knows? At least I'll be able to keep a little cash after I pay off all of these."

"Will half of what you're worth be enough to cover them?" Jake asked. "I assume whoever inherits Snappy's share of the business may be reluctant to part with any of their windfall."

"Fortunately, I don't need to find out. We had an understanding that if one of us should die, the other partner would get everything. Snappy was quite a bit older than me, so we both kind of assumed that he'd go first, but not for a whole lot of years, you know?"

"Was it drawn up in a legal document?" Jake asked him.

Bloch looked annoyed by the question. "We set our wills up in each other's favor. At the time, we figured we'd kill two birds with one stone. Sorry, that was probably a poor choice of words. I still can't believe that he's gone."

It was an interesting admission that the partners were each other's beneficiaries. Was Bloch telling us before we could find out on our own, or was it just casual conversation? I needed to find out, but before I could ask another question, he asked me one. "If you're not here for a refund, then why are you here?"

"We're looking into Snappy's murder," Jake said.

"Really. A donut maker and her bodyguard? Interesting."

"He's much more than a bodyguard," I said proudly. "Jake used to be with the state police."

"The key phrase in that sentence being 'used to be.' As a matter of fact, I've already spoken to the police, so there's nothing left for me to tell you." Bloch's phone rang, and after glancing at his caller ID, he said, "Sorry to cut this short, but I've got to take this."

We didn't have time to get in another word as he pointed to the door.

Once we were outside, Jake said, "Suzanne, you don't have to tell everyone we meet what I used to do for a living."

"Are you kidding? They're usually a lot more willing to talk to us if they know that than if they think you're just some random stranger tagging along with me."

"I hear what you're saying, but I hate using my old job as leverage," Jake explained.

"Okay. I get it."

"Does that mean you won't do it again?" he asked me.

"I can't honestly say. I suppose it depends on the circumstances. Can you live with that?"

"It doesn't sound as though I have much choice," he said with a crooked grin. "So how much do you think the business is worth?"

"Judging by the condition of that building, after he pays that stack of bills, he'll be lucky if he has enough for the stamp to mail in his taxes," I said.

"Maybe," Jake said. "I'd like to find out for sure, though."

"We could always call Momma and ask her," I suggested.

"How could she possibly know the answer to that?"

"Jake, the things my mother knows or can find out at a moment's notice continue to amaze me even to this day."

"She *is* pretty terrific," Jake agreed, and then he quickly added, "And so is her daughter, for that matter."

"We both thank you," I said. "Now, we need to find Snappy's son and then his girlfriend and see what they have to say."

"Sanderson is probably home right now accepting visitors," Jake said. "I took the liberty of doing a little preliminary work while you were getting ready, so I've got his address if you want to start with him."

"I didn't take that long on the phone before, did I?" I asked.

"No, but I'm just that good. Come on. Let's go check out his house."

We drove to the address Jake had found while I'd been on the phone earlier, and I prepared myself to brace a man who had just lost his father to a violent death. Whether they'd gotten along in life was irrelevant to me. The man had lost someone close to him, and I didn't expect him to be in very good emotional shape. I started to feel bad for him as we rang the doorbell, but that evaporated quickly.

A pretty redhead answered the door wearing only a man's

dress shirt, and from the mussed condition of her hair, I suspected that she'd been doing something a little more than mourning with Snappy Mack's son.

CHAPTER 4

"MAY I HELP YOU?" THE redhead asked us after we all just stood there for a moment.

"Are you Madison, by any chance?" I asked her.

"Yes, I'm Madison Moore," she said. "Who are you?"

"I'm Suzanne Hart, and this is my husband, Jake. We're here to see Sanderson and offer him our condolences," I said.

"Go on in. He's in the living room," she answered, and then she appeared to just realize what she was wearing. "Excuse me, but I spilled some wine on my dress, so Sandy was nice enough to loan me his shirt."

Sandy, was it? Under ordinary circumstances, it would have been a perfectly valid excuse.

I just didn't believe it.

"How sweet of him," I said.

"Anyway, you can go on in. I'm heading home to change."

"But you'll be back soon, right?" Jake asked her politely.

Madison sized him up in a second, and I felt myself bristle as the woman treated my husband as a piece of meat. "You can count on it."

I put my hand instinctively on Jake's arm, but if Madison noticed it, she didn't show it.

After she was gone, I told my husband in a soft voice, "Well, it appears that you've made yourself a new friend."

"Suzanne, we need her to like us."

"Agreed, but not too much, if you know what I mean."

Jake was robbed of the opportunity to respond as we entered the living room. There were flowers and plants all around, as well as stacks of food placed on the folding tables. "Our deepest condolences," I said as we approached him. I wished I'd made donuts so I could bring a gift of my own, but that hadn't been an option, not that I was blaming the victim for shutting down my shop.

I blamed the killer and the killer alone for that.

"Thank you," he said as he rose off the couch, shook our hands, and then sat heavily back down. I could see bits of his father in him, and I wondered how much he'd grow to resemble him in the future. "How did you know my father?"

"As a matter of fact, I was his last client," I said, hating myself instantly for the way it must have sounded to him.

"You own the donut shop," Sanderson said numbly.

"I had the privilege of spending some time with your father a few days ago," Jake said smoothly, bailing me out from my awkward comment. "He was a unique individual, wasn't he?" my husband asked Sanderson with a smile.

"That's putting it mildly," the man's son said with a partial grin. "I can't even imagine what he told you about me."

Jake shrugged. "We've all been there. Fathers can be hard on their sons. I know that from firsthand experience myself." Jake hadn't had the greatest of childhoods, but it was something he rarely talked about, even with me. Was he trying to soften Sanderson up, or was he genuinely sharing his experiences with the man in an effort to console him? I suddenly realized that there was no reason he couldn't be doing both things at the same time.

"What can I say? We just never seemed to manage to get along," Sanderson said.

"I must say, it surprised me to find Madison here," I said. "I just assumed that you two weren't all that close, based on your relationship with your dad."

"Believe it or not, Madison and I went to high school together," Sanderson said a little ruefully. "You can imagine how thrilled I was when my dad started going out with her."

"I hope she didn't ruin her dress," I said, looking to see if Sanderson would back up Madison's story.

"She said it would be fine," he replied absently. Maybe I'd jumped to conclusions earlier, and there really had been an accident. I would have loved to see that dress for myself to find out one way or the other, though. "I appreciate you stopping by."

It was a clear dismissal, but I wasn't ready to go quite just yet, though. "We just left Hank Bloch," I said. "Has he been by to see you yet?"

"Actually, I went by the shop myself this morning. I wanted to talk to him about my father's business holdings, but Hank insisted that we wait for the lawyers and the reading of Dad's will. I'm not sure how I'm going to feel being partnered with the man, given his temperament."

"Partners?" Jake asked softly.

"As my father's only living heir, it's just natural to assume that I'll be getting everything he owned, including his share of the business."

I was about to say something about what Hank Bloch had told us when Jake interrupted me. "We won't keep you, then. We just wanted to stop by and offer you our condolences."

I raised an eyebrow, but Jake barely shook his head. As we headed for the door, my husband paused and looked back at Sanderson Mack. "When did you see your father last, if you don't mind me asking?"

"I can't believe it, but it was just yesterday afternoon," Sanderson said. "That's what's so tragic about this. We'd finally managed to put our differences aside, and now this happens."

I thought they hadn't gotten along. Was he backpedaling from that statement after realizing how it must have sounded to us?

"At least you can take some solace from that," I said.

As Jake and I reached the door, the bell rang, and I found neighbors bearing food standing on the stoop. "Just put it in there," I said as I pointed to the kitchen, and then Jake and I walked out of the house.

Once we were outside, I asked my husband, "What was that all about? Why didn't you let me tell him that Hank Bloch has a completely different view on what happens to Snappy's possessions?"

"Think about it for a second, Suzanne. It gains us nothing by telling him. Let's see what he does when he finds out on his own."

"If Bloch was even right," I said. "It sounds as though it's about to be a real mess."

"Aren't you glad you're not involved with the will?" Jake asked me as a sports car drove up and parked near us.

"For more reasons than I can count," I said.

Madison got out, wearing a dress that was entirely too short for mourning, at least in my opinion.

She approached Jake and smiled. "This is much better, don't you think?" she asked as she twirled around for him.

"I don't know. The other outfit had its own merits, too," my husband said with a grin as he looked at me.

I pinched him out of Madison's sight.

"Are you leaving already?" she asked, clearly sounding disappointed with our coming absence. Could the woman not keep herself from flirting with any man within sight?

"Sorry, but we have to," I said. "That's a nice car you've got there."

She beamed at it. "Thanks. Isn't it super cute? It was a present from Snappy." Lowering her voice, she leaned in and asked us softly, "Can you keep a secret? I'm getting a great deal more than a car. Snappy made out a new will recently. I'm getting everything, including this house."

"Do you happen to have a copy of the will on you?" Jake asked. "I'd be interested in seeing it."

The stylish redhead looked puzzled by the request. "No, it's with my lawyers. Now, if you'll excuse me, I've got to go in and keep Sandy company."

"I understand you two went to school together," I said.

"Isn't that a hoot? I never dreamed I'd end up with his father. Well, I've got to go. Don't be strangers now, you hear?"

After Madison was back inside, Jake's frown blossomed. "Does *everyone* believe they're going to inherit Snappy's money?"

"It appears so," I said. "Were you flirting with Madison just then?"

"Is that why you pinched me? Suzanne, the woman clearly thrives on praise from men. If I'm nice to her, I'll be able to get more information out of her. I want the woman to try to please me."

I didn't like the sound of that at all, but I just shrugged in response, mainly because I had a hunch that Jake had read Madison perfectly and that I was just being silly.

Movement caught my eye from the house across the street, and I looked over and saw a middle-aged man standing in the window openly watching us.

"Where are you going?" Jake asked me as I started off across the street and away from his truck.

"I'm following up on a hunch," I said. I expected the neighbor to retreat, but to my surprise, he came out of the house as we approached instead.

"Excuse me, sir. Do you have a second?"

"That's *all* I seem to have these days. What can I do for you?" The man was clearly eager to chat.

"You don't miss much of the comings and goings over there, do you?" I asked him with a grin as I glanced back at Sanderson's, or more likely Snappy's, house.

He answered with a shrug. "What can I say? I like to think of myself as our very own neighborhood watch."

"Do you keep close tabs on what goes on over there?" I asked him.

"There's not much else I *can* do since I got laid off. Television bores me, I have trouble reading, but I love seeing the world go by outside my window. It doesn't help matters that I can't seem to sleep at night. I'm getting a few hours of rest during the day, but there's something about the dark that keeps me awake."

"I bet a lot's been going on across the street lately," I said.

"You mean Madison's nocturnal visits?" he asked with a grin. "Yes, she's been a frequent visitor over there, even before Sanderson's dad died." It was clear he liked nothing more than sharing a bit of gossip with us, but his phone rang inside, and as he dashed back in, he said, "I've got to take this call. It's about a job interview."

With that, he slammed the door in our faces.

Jake looked at me and grinned. "That happens a lot to you, doesn't it?"

"Getting doors slammed in my face? More than I'd care to admit," I replied. "Let's get back to Snappy's will. There has to be one true final version. The real question is, who has it?"

"It sounds as though we need to ask around and see if we can find out," Jake replied. "It could be the key to solving this case."

That sounded like something a lawyer might be able to help us with, and there was only one attorney I knew in Maple Hollow.

It was time to go see Adam Jefferson.

"Turn left here," I ordered Jake as we got to a more familiar part of town.

"That's odd. I figured the attorney's office would either be downtown or near the courthouse," Jake replied as he drove as I'd directed him.

"It is. I want to see my aunt's house."

"I get it," he said. Jake slowed down when he got near it.

"Pull over and stop right here."

Momma had been right. I wouldn't have made the same choices the new owners had in cutting the trees back and the bushes completely down, but it certainly let in more light than it had when Aunt Jean had owned the house. The large and somewhat ancient Victorian had gotten a facelift since I'd last seen it, and I had a feeling that my aunt would have approved of at least that part of it.

"You can drive now," I said.

"We could always knock on the front door and ask the new owner if we could look around," my husband suggested.

"Thanks, but I'm not sure I could take it. I just wanted to see it one last time. Now I never need to come back. Just drive the way you came in, and we'll be at the attorney's office in no time." I knew that Jake wanted to say something, so I added quickly, "I'm fine. Really. Let's forget about the past for the moment and concentrate on our investigation. That's all right with you, isn't it?"

"Yes, of course it is. You know, if Adam Jefferson is representing anyone in this estate, he's not going to be able to tell us anything."

"I get that, but it's still worth a shot, isn't it?"

"Right now, it's as good a lead as any," Jake said. He found space near the attorney's office, and after parking the truck, we went inside.

"Do you even *own* a suit?" I asked the attorney with a smile when he greeted us. He was dressed much as he had been when we'd first met, faded blue jeans and an old DUKE sweatshirt.

"I do, but I seem to wear this more often," he replied as he shook our hands. "I don't recommend owning rental property to anyone, even though I know it's a sound financial move. What they don't tell you is how much work it's going to be."

"I get that completely," Jake said. He'd met the attorney briefly, but I was our main contact with the man.

I asked him, "Adam, do you have a minute? We're looking for some free advice."

He grinned at me. "And you came to an *attorney*?"

"What can I say? We figured it was worth a shot," I admitted.

"Wow, you must be desperate. Sure, I'll help you if I can. What's up?"

"Snappy Mack was working at my donut shop when he was murdered," I said. After all, there was no sense beating around the bush.

"I heard," the attorney said somberly. "Sorry about that."

"It's not your fault," I said. "Did you represent him?"

"If I did, I couldn't discuss his situation with you," Adam said.

"So then, is that a no?" Jake asked him.

"Snappy and I never really hit it off. The man played his cards close to the chest, which I can completely respect, but when I found out he was withholding vital information from me a few years ago and I called him on it, he fired me on the spot. Not before paying me in full, at any rate, and you'd better believe I got his check before I let him walk out the door. What specifically did you want to know about him?"

"Everyone seems to be fighting over his estate," I told him, "but from what we've seen, it's not going to amount to much. Why all the fuss?"

"Who do you mean when you say 'everyone'?" he asked me.

"Funny, I thought I was asking the questions," I reminded him.

"You can ask away, but there needs to be a little quid pro quo here, since I'm off the clock."

I glanced at Jake, who nodded his approval. I told him, "So far, we've spoken with Madison Moore, Hank Bloch, and Snappy's son, Sanderson, and all three of them are under the impression that they'll be inheriting the bulk of the man's estate."

"Now why doesn't that surprise me?" Adam asked with a grin. "Snappy had a habit of overpromising things. Do you think one of them had something to do with his murder?"

"It's entirely possible, I'm sorry to say," I said.

Adam frowned a moment before he spoke again. "All three of them have mean streaks; I can tell you that much. I'm puzzled by one thing, though. You didn't mention Deloris."

"Who exactly is Deloris?" Jake asked, jotting the name down carefully in his little notebook. It had been a habit of his when he'd been with the state police, and he still carried one wherever he went.

"Deloris Mack, Snappy's wife," the attorney explained. "Ex-wife, I should say."

"Is she Sanderson's mother?" I asked.

"No, that was Janine. She died when Sanderson was a teenager, and Snappy married Deloris not long after he buried his first wife. Tongues wagged, or so I've heard."

"Is Deloris still in town?" I asked.

"Oh, yes. She owns a little shop in town that sells candles. I don't know how she makes a living doing it, but she seems to squeak by. You should speak with her. I'm guessing she, too, is going to think she's coming into some money, if I knew Snappy."

"Getting back to our original question," Jake said, "is there even going to be any money to distribute after his bills are all paid?"

The attorney whistled softly to himself. "You'd better believe it."

"Seriously? We were just at Snappy's office, and it's not much."

"The man had a great deal more than just his construction business. He's been buying up dilapidated old properties for years on the side, rehabbing them, and then renting them out and making a fortune."

"How much are we talking about here?" I asked him, surprised to hear the new information.

"If I had to guess, I'd say that it could be in the neighborhood of three million. Then again, it could be more, but probably not much less."

I looked at him, stunned to hear the news. "I'm having a hard time believing that."

"I know. It's really true what they say; you can't judge a book by its cover." Adam was about to add something else when his phone rang. "Excuse me for one second." He took the call, and after identifying himself, he mostly listened. "Yes. Of course. I understand. Fine. That works for me. I'd be happy to. See you then."

"Who was that?" I asked out of curiosity more than a need to know.

"Unfortunately, I'm not at liberty to discuss that anymore, nor can I offer any further speculation about Snappy Mack's real or imagined net worth. Thanks for stopping by," he said as he shook each of our hands, and then he added, "It was good seeing you again, Suzanne. I keep meaning to make it to the donut shop, but something always seems to come up."

"Like one of our suspects hiring you to represent them on the spot, you mean?" I asked him with a grin.

"No comment," he replied, smiling just as broadly back at me.

Once we were outside again, Jake looked at me. "So, which one of them do you think it was on the other end of that phone call?"

"I have no idea," I said, "but unless I miss my guess, things are about to get ugly in Maple Hollow."

CHAPTER 5

"Excuse me, are you Mrs. Mack?" I asked as we walked into Wax and Wicks, Snappy's ex-wife's deserted candle shop. It was a cutesy kind of place, featuring candles of all shapes and sizes prominently displayed, along with blocks of wax and a variety of molds and wicks. There were even a few electric candles, their flickering wicks beating time to the music playing in the background. The woman behind the counter was younger than I'd been expecting but still a stark contrast to Snappy's current love. While Madison was young, pretty, and more than a little perky, this woman wore her gray hair proudly down her back and looked like an enhanced picture of Mother Earth. She sported a multicolored muumuu and sandals that appeared to have been made on some Caribbean island, and she had a solid weight about her that went beyond her stature.

"I prefer Deloris," she said. "I consider Mack to be my indentured name."

"I take it you weren't a big fan of your ex-husband's," I said.

"On the contrary. Snappy and I made much better friends than we ever did spouses. I just can't believe he's gone."

"If you were still close, I'm surprised that you're still open, and not at Sanderson's place commiserating with his friends and family," I said. Jake was staying in the background for this interview, so I was running with it full steam ahead.

"The truth of the matter is that the little snot is not my

37

biggest fan," Deloris said as she bit her lower lip. "I won't be surprised if he tries to bar me from the funeral, but let him try! If he's itching for a fight, then I'm just the gal to give it to him. Now that his father is gone, there's no reason for me to hold back any longer."

The declaration of war didn't match the woman's outward appearance, and I had to wonder if she'd really been as close to Snappy as she and Adam Jefferson had claimed.

Then her face softened for a moment as she added, "If I didn't have to pay the bills, I would have shut things down in a heartbeat. After all, it's hard to say when the will is going to be read and when all of that takes effect. It could be several months before I get my inheritance."

"Let me guess," Jake said from behind me. "You're his main beneficiary."

"How did you know?" she asked him. "Snappy always promised to look out for me once he was gone. I just wish it hadn't happened so soon."

This was getting ridiculous. "Deloris, do you have any idea how many people are under the impression that *they're* his primary beneficiaries?"

"They can believe anything they'd like," she said with ultimate confidence. "I've got the paperwork to back my position up."

I glance over at Jake, who merely replied, "If I were you, I'd check the date on that document. There's a possibility that someone else has a more recent claim on the estate, and the last will written is the one that will be enforced."

Deloris's face went white at the news. "Snappy wouldn't do that to me."

"He wouldn't?" I asked her softly. "How can you be so sure?"

"But that changes everything. I *need* that inheritance." She was clearly distraught by the prospect of being written out of her ex-husband's will.

"Needing it and receiving it can be two very different things," Jake told her.

Deloris looked truly troubled now. "I need to see what's going on. If you'll excuse me…" she said as she literally tried to push us out the door.

"We just have a few more questions," I said, but it turned out to be of no avail.

Before we knew what was happening, Jake and I were standing on the sidewalk in front of the candle shop, and all of the lights inside were going out en masse.

"Is there *anyone* in town Snappy didn't promise to leave his money to?" I asked Jake as we headed back to his truck.

"I don't know about you, but I'm starting to feel a little left out. We're in the minority, because as far as I know, we were never mentioned in any of the many versions of the man's last will and testament, whatever the last version ends up being," Jake said with a rueful shrug. "What an idiot!"

"How so?" I asked.

"Think about it, Suzanne. Snappy gave at least four people a motive to want to see him dead, all by bragging about how much they were going to get from his estate when he died. It was almost as though he was *begging* to be murdered."

"You don't believe that, do you?" I asked my husband softly.

"No. Of course not. It just doesn't make our job any easier, does it? Every last one of our suspects believes they are going to receive the bulk of the man's estate. When the others discover who really gets it, the final beneficiary is the one who's going to need an insurance policy."

"If solving murder cases was that easy, everybody would be doing it," I said with a grin. I glanced at my watch and noticed that it was just past eleven. Where had the morning gone? "Are you hungry?"

"I am. I was just about to mention it to you. I don't know how you feel, but I don't want to wait until we get back to April Springs to eat something. Do you know of any good places we can eat around here?"

I thought about the time Momma and I had spent in town, and I remembered one particular café immediately. "There's a place called Burt's not far from here that's not bad," I said. "Plus, it has the added bonus of being a hub of the town's gossip center. You can bet folks are talking about what happened to Snappy in my donut shop this morning. Who knows? Maybe we'll get lucky and overhear something that's helpful to our investigation."

"And even if we don't learn anything new, at least we'll get to eat," Jake said. "Just tell me where I need to go."

I laughed despite the serious nature of our task. "I can't tell you how long I've been waiting to hear you say that."

"If I were you, I wouldn't get used to it," Jake replied.

"What can I say? Where there's life, there's hope."

"Welcome to Burt's," the familiar waitress said as Jake and I walked into the café. "Hey, I know you," she said when she spied me standing behind my husband.

"Hey, Tammy, how are you?"

"I couldn't be better if I won the lottery," the middle-aged woman with short blonde hair and granny glasses said. In a softer voice, she added, "We all know that's a big fat lie, but since the boss is watching, it wouldn't do to advertise the fact. Two for lunch?"

"Please," I said as she led us to a table.

"What's good here?" Jake inquired, something he always asked whenever he ate someplace new. It had yielded some surprisingly good recommendations over the years, along with a few clunkers as well from time to time.

"You can't go wrong with today's special," Tammy said, her pencil poised over her order pad.

"That sounds good to me," Jake said with a grin as he handed the menu back to her without even glancing at it.

"Don't you even want to know what you'll be having?"

"What can I say? I like to live dangerously. Surprise me."

Tammy laughed and then turned to me. "How about you?"

"We might as well both have it."

"I like you two," she said as she jotted our orders down. "You're my kind of people. I'll bring you a pair of sweet teas, since that's our best drink, if that's okay with you."

"Why not? We're in it all the way," Jake said.

Tammy winked at me. "Suzanne, I believe that you found yourself a keeper there."

"Don't I know it, but don't say it too loudly. I'd hate for it to go to his head."

"I can hear you just fine," Jake told us, clearly bemused by the turn our conversation had taken. "You both know that, don't you?"

"Don't pay us any mind," Tammy said. "I'll be right back in two shakes and a wiggle."

After she'd gone to get us our drinks, Jake said, "She's one of a kind, isn't she?"

"She's different, all right. You want to know something? I think you're pretty special, too," I said as I patted his hand. "I may not say it enough, but my life's a lot more fun with you than it ever was without you."

"I totally agree with that," Jake replied as he looked around.

I looked at him closely as I asked, "Does that mean you understand that my life is better with you or that yours is better with me in it?"

He laughed. "Yes. To both questions. Here's our food. It may not be great, but at least it's fast."

As Tammy served us, I asked her, "Have you heard about Snappy Mack?"

"Are you kidding? It's all the town's talking about."

"It happened in my shop, Tammy," I said softly, "and we aim to find out who did it. Can you give us a hand?" I was taking a chance trusting the waitress, but after all, I couldn't go through life trusting only the folks I knew to the core. Being suspicious of everyone I met was no way to live, and I wasn't going to settle for that watered-down version of life.

"I might," she said grimly as she looked around to see who might be watching us. "Give me a minute and I'll get back to you on that." In a much louder voice, she added, "You two enjoy your food now, you hear?"

"We plan to," I said just as loudly.

I looked over at Jake to see that his fork was poised over the mashed potatoes. He was doing his best not to smile and failing miserably at it.

"What are you grinning about?" I asked him.

"That was smooth. I like the way you talk to people, Suzanne."

"I'm not doing anything all that special. I just open my mouth, and the words seem to spill out," I said, cutting off a bite of the country-style steak and brushing it through the gravy. "Man, that's tasty."

Jake tried his as well and smiled. "Nice. I'd hate to know the calorie content of this meal, but whatever it is, it's worth every bite."

As we ate and chatted, we tried to keep our conversation off the contractor and his recent demise. Most of the time during our meal we spent listening to the idle speculation going on around us about who might have done it. It was reassuring that the main names I heard belonged to folks we already suspected of the crime, not that diner gossip anywhere could always be believed.

"Anyone want dessert?" Tammy asked as she came back to check on us. "We've got some fresh pie that's delicious, and some cake that's seen better days, but it still might be okay if you're really feeling daring."

"I'm stuffed," I said as I pushed my plate away, "but feel free to have something if you'd like, Jake."

"No, I'd better take a pass as well. We'll just take the check, please."

I started to say something when Tammy put it down in front of me before I could add another question about Snappy. I wasn't sure how things worked in the rest of the country, but in the South, the men *always* got the bill first. If there was any splitting or divvying going on after that, it normally happened *after* the waitress left.

As a matter of habit, Jake started to reach for the bill automatically when Tammy said, "It's been a pleasure."

On a hunch, I flipped the ticket over and saw that there was a yellow sticky note attached to the bill. It said, "*Talk to Meredith at the library.*"

I pulled the sticky note off and handed the bill to Jake. "Thanks for lunch," I said as I folded the note once and tucked it into my jeans pocket.

"My pleasure," he said.

When we got to the register, Tammy was gone, though I half expected to see her there waiting for us, but she was nowhere to be found.

Jake asked the cashier, "Can you cash a hundred? I don't know why the banks insist on giving them when you cash a check."

"I do," the woman up front said. "After all, it's a lot easier to count out one bill than it is five or ten. Don't worry, we mostly run a cash business here, so it won't be a problem."

Jake stuffed the twenties and odd ones into his wallet, and we walked outside into the brisk January wind.

"I thought Tammy would be out here waiting for us, but she's nowhere in sight," I said as I finally gave up my search scanning the café's parking lot.

"Clearly she didn't want anyone seeing us together," Jake said. "I get it. Tensions are probably running pretty high around town right now. Do you know this Meredith woman at the library?"

"Our paths crossed a few times during my investigation of Aunt Jean's murder," I admitted. "She's good people."

"Then let's go have a chat with her, shall we?"

CHAPTER 6

"MEREDITH, DO YOU HAVE A second? Do you remember me?" The librarian hadn't changed much since I'd last seen her, tall and thin with the same wispy blonde hair, though her eyes were red from something. Jake had held back to allow me to get reacquainted and approach her on my own, at least at first.

"I'm not likely to ever forget you. How have you been, Suzanne?"

"All in all, I've been fine. You?"

"What can I say? The books come in and the books go out, but less and less of them every month." She waved a hand around the nearly deserted space. A few folks were reading newspapers on long bamboo poles, there were at least four people napping in the warmth of the space, and one older woman was sitting quietly, knitting of all things, without a book in sight. "We're trying to expand our ebook collection, but it's a brave new world, isn't it?"

"The way I look at it, reading is reading, whether it's on paper, an ereader, a cell phone, or even if it's written in the mud with a stick."

"It would be difficult loaning those out," she said with a laugh, "but I agree with your point. Now, what brings you to my library?"

"We were just speaking with Tammy at Burt's," I started when the librarian cut me off.

"You should know that you can believe about a third of what Tammy says. The trick is in knowing which third," Meredith said.

"She told us we should speak with you about Snappy Mack's death."

"Murder, you mean," Meredith said with a frown. "Why on earth are you interested in his demise?"

It managed to surprise me that word hadn't gotten completely out, even though he hadn't been found all that long ago. "It happened in my donut shop. That makes it personal in my book," I admitted, something that gave me great discomfort.

"I'm so sorry," she said instantly. "I heard he was killed on a job site in April Springs, but I didn't put it together with you. Are you okay?"

"Not yet, but I will be. By the way, that man over there pretending not to notice us is my husband, Jake."

"Well, he certainly doesn't have to avoid being with us on my account. Bring him over."

I motioned to Jake, and he came immediately. After introductions, I asked the librarian, "Why did Tammy think you might be of some assistance to us?"

"Oh, I thought she might have said something to you about why I care so much about what happened to Snappy. You see, he was my uncle."

"Your what?" I asked a little too loudly for the woman knitting. She shushed me, frowned, and then went back to her project. "Sorry about that," I added in a softer voice. "I'm so sorry for your loss."

"Thank you. Snappy and I were close when I was growing up, but a distance had grown between us over the years. I'm pleased to say that all changed over the last four months. My uncle, never someone you could call a big reader, suddenly discovered the joy of books. It's never too late, if you ask me, and we had a dozen late-night conversations about what he should read next. I'm sorry he's gone, but at least we had that much to share in the end."

"Do you have any idea who might want to see harm come to him?" I asked her.

"Do I ever. I could make you a list," she said.

Jake asked her softly, "Would it include Sanderson, Madison, Deloris, and Hank?"

She looked at him as though he'd just grown another head. "Who exactly are you?"

"I figured she told you. I'm Suzanne's husband," he patiently explained.

"I already know that," Meredith said dismissively. "What I'm talking about is, *who* are you?"

"I understand the question," I said. "Jake is a retired state police inspector, and once upon a time, he was also the chief of police for April Springs."

"But not in that order, I presume."

"No, it happened in exactly that order," I said. "Since your uncle died in my shop, I feel obligated to find out what happened to him."

"We already know that, though, don't we? Unless you believe that screwdriver wasn't the fatal blow."

I forgot I was speaking with a librarian, a woman who prided herself on her clear communication and the importance of words and their usage.

"What I meant to say earlier was that we want to find out *who* killed him."

"I only wish I could help, but you've just named every suspect I can think of. Please find out who murdered Snappy, Suzanne. We lost so much time over the years that it's criminal he was taken just when we'd managed to find a way to reconnect."

"We'll do our best," I said. "It was great seeing you, Meredith."

"And you as well. Don't be strangers, though I suspect that shop of yours keeps you busy most of the time."

"You have no idea," I said with a smile.

Once we were outside, Jake asked, "I have a question that I'm pretty sure you aren't going to like."

"Fire away," I said.

"Could *she* have done it?"

The idea shocked me. "Who, Meredith? No."

"What exactly are you basing that on?" Jake wondered aloud. "Your emotions?"

"It's not my heart telling me that she didn't do it, it's my gut. Meredith is mourning her uncle, and unless you can produce video showing her plunging that screwdriver into the man's back, I'm going to continue believing that she's innocent."

"Because she's so likeable?" Jake asked me softly. He was testing me, and what's more, I knew it.

"No, we both know that killers can be extremely likeable sometimes," I said. "If I have to quantify it, I couldn't begin to do so. All I know is that she's not on my list until I find out something that says otherwise."

Jake nodded. "That's good enough for me, then. Just remember, we both need to keep an open mind though, no matter how much we might personally like a suspect." After a moment, he added, "She's about the *only* one likeable in the group, isn't she? Snappy Mack certainly surrounded himself with some unlikeable people."

"It sure seems that way to me," I said. "What do we do now?" After a moment, I grabbed my husband's arm and pulled him behind a tree.

"If you want to kiss me in the bushes, I heartily approve,

but aren't we a little too old to be acting like teenagers?" he asked me.

"Shh," I said as I pointed to someone approaching the library on foot.

It was the chief of police for Maple Hollow, and I was going to do my best to duck Chief Kessler if there was any way I could manage it.

Jake and I stood there in the shadows of the trees, and after the police chief passed us and went inside, I said, "You know what? This might be a good time to go back home."

"Why, because of the chief?" Jake asked. "He knows why we're here, Suzanne."

"Yes, but that doesn't necessarily mean that he approves of what we're doing," I said.

"Still, it's no reason for us to run and hide."

"Jake, I know this goes against your grain, but we don't want to rouse the man's ire if we don't have to. Why do you think he's going to the library? Does he look like a big reader to you? I'm willing to bet that he's going to talk to Meredith, and if he does, our names are going to come up."

"So? We haven't done anything illegal," Jake said stubbornly.

"No, but we also don't have any more clues to chase down here, do we? Unless you want to go by Snappy's place and look around, that is."

"Of course I do," Jake said. "I was a cop too long not to believe in the power of physical evidence. I don't have any idea where Snappy lived though, do you?"

"No, but we can always find out," I said, reaching for my phone.

"Who are you calling?" Jake asked me.

"One of the best sources of information I know," I said. "I'm calling Momma."

"Do you think she'll know?"

"Maybe not, but odds are good that she can find out quicker than we can," I said as I hit my speed-dial.

Momma laughed when she heard my request.

"What's so funny?" I asked her.

"Phillip assumed you'd be calling for that bit of information, so he's already tracked it down for you."

"Thank him for me, would you?" I asked. "Where did Snappy live?"

"You're not going to believe this. Well, maybe you will, given what you've no doubt found out already. The place Sanderson is staying is in Snappy's name, but he's never lived there. It appears Snappy recently sold his main residence for a healthy profit and banked the cash. In the meantime, he's been staying somewhere else."

"Please don't tell me it was with Madison Moore," I said. I wasn't sure I was ready to expose my husband to the woman again so soon.

"No, and he wasn't staying with his son, either."

"I give up, then," I said, growing tired of the game we were playing. "Where was Snappy staying?"

"Apparently there's an apartment above the office, so that's where he's been living for the past two weeks," Momma said.

"The office? You're kidding."

"I wish I were, but it seems that's what really happened. There's a small bachelor pad up there, and that's where he's been living."

"Thanks for finding that out, and thank Phillip for us as well."

"How is your investigation going?" Momma asked hesitantly.

"You know how it is. The first part is usually the toughest. We're still in the fact-gathering stages."

"Well, take care of Jake, and have him do the same for you," my overprotective mother said as if it were a memorized line spouted at each and every opportunity.

"You bet," I said.

Jake looked at me with a grin after I told him the news. "He's been staying at the office? Really?"

"Actually, there's supposedly an apartment on the second floor, but I have no idea how we're going to get in there to search the place, not with Hank Bloch working below it."

"Maybe there's an outside entrance that doesn't go up through the shop," Jake suggested.

"Hang on. Am I hearing this correctly? Are you actually willing to break in without first getting someone's permission to search the place?"

"Suzanne, can you imagine for one second that both police chiefs haven't already searched that place intensely? The least we can do is check it out while we're here."

"I'm thrilled you're finally coming over to the dark side," I said with a smile as we got into the truck and started driving back to the construction company.

"I haven't done anything I shouldn't have," Jake said a little too stiffly for my taste. I wasn't about to let him get away with that.

"Yet, you mean," I asked as I tweaked his arm lightly.

"Yet," he agreed with the hint of a grin.

Jake was clearly right.

There was a rear stairwell behind the building that no doubt led up to Snappy Mack's apartment.

There was only one problem, though.

The police tape across the bottom of the stairs might have been made from flimsy plastic, easy to cut with the dullest of knives, but for Jake, it may as well have been impenetrable steel.

That was one line that he was not about to cross.

"I don't suppose you'd wait for me while I ducked under the tape and checked it out for myself, would you?"

"Sorry. That's not going to happen," he said in a voice that allowed no debate. If it had been Grace and me working together, I would have probably done it anyway, but though Jake brought his own particular enormous set of skills to my investigation, he was still a tad too law abiding for my taste.

It appeared that we'd have to wait to get permission to search Snappy's bachelor pad later, and that wasn't going to happen anytime soon.

CHAPTER 7

WE HAD BEEN ON THE road five minutes heading back to April Springs when my cell phone rang, and it was a number I didn't recognize. "Hello?"

"Is this Suzanne Hart?" the voice on the other end asked. It was a gruff man, and if I had to guess, I'd say that he was somewhere easily past middle age.

"Speaking." I waited for him to fill me in as to why he was calling, but there was just an extended time of silence. "May I help you with something?" I asked him.

"Sorry, I was finishing up a bid and I had to jot a few numbers down before I forgot them. The name's Young. Your mother arranged for me to work on your donut shop, and it turns out we can fit you in sooner than we first thought. How's tomorrow work for you?"

"Tomorrow sounds great," I said, excited about the prospect of getting Donut Hearts back to its former glory, or at least as much of it as I could currently afford.

Before I could say another word, he broke in. "Listen, I know it might not be convenient for you, but I need to meet you there tomorrow morning so we can go over the work that needs to be done. The best time of day for me is seven a.m." He said it as though he were expecting a fight from me. Well, he was going to get one, but not the kind he thought.

"I'm really sorry, but seven won't work," I said.

"I know it's early, but I'm going to have to order supplies, take measurements, and make arrangements with my crew before we start working. Surely you can push your schedule a little for that."

"I was about to say that seven is much too late for me," I explained with a great deal of satisfaction. "Five would be much better for me."

"In the morning?"

"It's the best time to get my undivided attention," I told him.

Mr. Young seemed surprised by my response but only for a few seconds. "I can make five work," he said, though he clearly thought I'd lost my mind. "Your mother said the actual work couldn't start until after one p.m. Is that right?"

"Sorry, but I'm going to need to keep my work schedule if I'm going to pay for the repairs," I said. "The insurance is probably going to cover some of it, but there's still going to be a substantial amount left after that. You want to get paid, don't you?"

He ignored my question and went straight to one of his own. "But after one, no one will be there, is that right?"

"Just you and your crew," I said.

The contractor hesitated again, and then he asked, "Just out of curiosity, how much did Snappy get finished?"

"Not much, but then again, he wasn't on the job very long," I admitted.

"That figures. Well, this won't be the first mess Snappy ever made that I had to clean up."

"Are you saying that he wasn't very good at his job?"

The contractor hesitated, and then he must have thought better of speaking ill of the dead. "Strike that. The whole thing's just got me a little jumpy. If you ask me, it's a bad sign when folks start killing contractors on the jobsite."

"You're not implying that *I* had anything to do with Snappy's murder, are you?" I asked him. I hoped this man was good with his hands, because his people skills needed some serious work.

"No, ma'am. Not at all. Anyway, I'll see you at five tomorrow. Just to confirm, that was a.m. and not p.m., right?"

"Right," I said.

After I hung up, Jake said, "I didn't even need to hear the other side of that conversation to know that man isn't going to be easy to work with. I can't believe you didn't fire him on the spot."

"Momma found him, so I don't really have much choice. I might as well give him a try."

Jake nodded, and then he drove a little farther down the road before he asked, "Did he actually come right out and accuse you of murder?"

"It's not important," I said, trying not to get riled up for no reason.

"Got it," Jake said, getting it immediately. We drove mostly in silence for the rest of the ride back to April Springs, and when Jake pulled into town, he asked me, "What's our game plan now?"

"I have no idea," I said, and as I did, I realized that it was true. We'd spoken with the main suspects on our list, and we'd even added one more name to it, but I didn't feel as though we were a single step closer to figuring out who had killed Snappy Mack. "Do you have any suggestions?"

For some odd reason, Jake seemed surprised that I'd ask him for advice. After a moment, he said, "I have an idea, but you're probably not going to like it."

"Try me. You never know," I said.

"Let's stop by the grocery store, get some ingredients for a nice meal, and cook it together at the cottage," Jake said.

"What good will that do us?"

"Suzanne, investigating isn't always about pushing forward. Sometimes you need to take a beat and let your subconscious catch up with you."

"Is that what this meal is supposed to do?" I asked.

"No, that's entirely because I'm getting hungry again," he answered with a grin.

"Already?"

"Hey, we ate a long time ago. Besides, I can't control when I want to eat. What do you say?"

"It sounds great to me," I admitted after realizing that there was really nothing else we could do at the moment. "What do you feel like making tonight?"

"It's not so much the making that I'm interested in as it is the eating," he said with a laugh.

"Okay. I'll bite. What do you feel like eating?"

"I figure some nice steaks, baked potatoes, green beans, bread, and some banana pudding for dessert might be nice."

I had to laugh at my husband's predictable response. I could have probably named all of the items on his wish list if he'd given me a handful of guesses, but the only sure one would have been the banana pudding. My husband's grandmother had always made him a special bowl of it for special occasions when he'd been a boy, and it was still one of his favorite desserts. "Let's go by the store and stock up, then," I said.

"I'll cook the steaks if you handle the rest," Jake said as we came out of the parking lot of the grocery store, our arms laden with bags.

"I wouldn't have it any other way," I said. Outdoor cooking seemed to be his domain, unless he was making his chili. Truth be told, I was happy he hadn't mentioned making that. Jake's chili could take the paint right off the side of a barn, and I was in no mood to have my mouth lit up like a fireworks display. "Won't you be freezing if you cook outside, though?"

"You know me. I love grilling out when it's cold. What I

can't understand are the folks who do it when it's ninety degrees out. If you ask me, the time to grill out is when the temperature is under forty. That way you have a fire to warm up at and you cook your food at the same time."

"Have I told you lately what an odd bird you are?" I asked him affectionately.

"It takes one to know one," he answered with a grin.

The meal was wonderful, and not just because I got to share it with my husband. He had the touch when it came to grilling steaks, something not even every steakhouse could claim.

"It's early still," Jake said after we finished cleaning up the dishes and polishing off dessert. I'd made some peach cobbler earlier in the week, so after the banana pudding was gone, we polished off the remnants of the cobbler on the pretense of wanting to wash the dish I'd made it in. It was really cozy eating with two forks across from each other. "Would you like to take a walk before it gets dark?" Jake suggested. We'd reached the shortest day of daylight we'd see, and sunshine was slowly creeping back into our lives, but it was at a maddeningly slow pace. Because of that, Jake and I were doing our best to take advantage of what little sun we seemed to get. I didn't know how folks made it through the winters in Alaska, and I knew that I'd never find out. There was too much North Carolina in this girl to ever relocate, especially across so many time zones.

Something had been nagging me since we'd left town that morning, and the longer I waited to address it, the more unsettled I'd become. "Jake, would you mind if I walked over to Donut Hearts for a bit?"

"Hang on a second. I'd be happy to go with you as soon as I finish putting the silverware away."

I hugged my husband as I said, "As much as I appreciate the

offer, I'd kind of like to go by myself. I'm going to be making donuts in not that many hours, and it's going to be jarring enough as it is remembering Snappy's body lying there in the middle of the floor. Maybe if I have a little time there alone this evening, I'll be able to accept it enough in the morning to be able to function. You're not angry with me, are you?"

"There's no way that's ever going to happen, Suzanne. I get it. Call me if you need me. I'll be right here."

I kissed him soundly. "Thanks for understanding."

"What can I say?" he asked with a grin. "I'm an understanding guy."

Walking out the door, I zipped my jacket against the cold wind that had recently come on. I knew in my heart that it was January, but it was still hard to accept the presence of so much chilly weather. While this was still better than the ice storm we'd recently gone through, I longed for the past days of autumn when all I needed was a light jacket.

The park was silent as dusk began to approach in a method that felt entirely premature to me, and I blew a little warm air into my hands as I walked. If I was going to keep taking these strolls through the park in the winter, I was going to have to start wearing gloves more often.

It was a short walk, and as I approached Donut Hearts, my gaze went directly to the scarred elements of the building: the patched walls and roof, the Plexiglas window out front, and the remnants of where my awning used to be, still partially attached to the side of the building.

After unlocking the door, stepping inside, and locking it back behind me, I realized that I'd never turned the heat back on. Flipping on the lights as I went, I got to the thermostat and turned it up, waiting for the old furnace to kick on. I swore to myself that from then on, I'd keep the heat on a little higher throughout the evening and the nighttime hours, even when I wasn't going to be there. At least the furnace worked. I was rewarded with warmth soon enough, and then I let myself take in what Snappy Mack had been up to. I hadn't had a chance to evaluate his progress earlier, my gaze being mostly riveted to his dead body at the time of its discovery.

What had the man been doing? For some reason unbeknownst to me, Snappy had gone well past the damaged parts of the wall and had destroyed entirely new sections, areas that had been untouched by the falling tree that had damaged the structure. Had the man completely lost his mind, or was he making more work for himself so he could bill me for more hours of labor? I took out my cell phone and turned on the flashlight app, shining it into the cavities that had been freshly exposed.

There was nothing to see, though, with the single exception of a piece of fragile old newspaper tucked behind the plaster adjoining a pristine section of the wall.

What was going on? Had they used the newspaper as a backer of some sort in the old days? I tried to pull it out to see if it matched what I'd seen on the floor earlier, the bloodstained section I'd stepped across when I'd found Snappy's body, but it wouldn't budge.

Was that why the contractor had pulled more of the wall away than had been strictly necessary?

I stood there staring at it for a full minute before I did something I never dreamed I'd be capable of doing.

I took a long, flat knife from the kitchen and used it to pry out the bit of plaster where the newspaper was stuck so I could free it.

To my surprise, a large section of plaster slipped free of the wall and landed on the concrete floor with a loud crash.

I hadn't meant to vandalize such a large section of wall,

but I didn't take a single moment to mourn what I'd just unwittingly done.

I looked down in shock at what had suddenly been revealed to me, something that hadn't seen the light of day in probably close to a hundred years.

CHAPTER 8

"J AKE, YOU NEED TO COME to the donut shop."

"What's going on, Suzanne?" he asked. "Is something wrong?"

"That depends on how you look at it," I said. "I need you to see something, and I wouldn't ask you to come if it weren't important."

"Don't touch anything. I'm on my way."

I started to put my cell phone away, and then I switched on the flashlight app and looked into the newly exposed cavity again. I wanted to pull the newspapers out to see everything that had been buried in them, but at the last second I decided to honor Jake's request and not do anything until he got there. It seemed to take him forever to show up, and when I finally heard his truck pull up outside, I wondered if it wouldn't have been faster if he'd just walked over from the house.

I met him at the door and saw that he had pulled his service revolver out.

"No worries. It's not that kind of thing," I told him, and he put the weapon away.

"Sorry. Force of habit, I guess."

"Don't apologize. Someday you might save my life with one of those habits of yours."

Jake looked around and saw the fresh chunk of plaster from the wall that was now residing on the concrete floor. "Doing a little remodeling on our own, are we?"

I led him to where I'd pulled the plaster off and pointed my phone's light in the cavity. "Look in there."

"It looks like more old newspaper to me," Jake said, dismissing my find out of hand.

"That's not what I'm pointing at," I said as I pulled the papers out and played my light into the opening. In the base of the wall opening, several faceted reflections glittered back at me. I'd caught a few glimpses of what had been hidden away, but now I could see them in their full glory.

"What are those?" Jake asked as he knelt down to take a closer look.

I started to reach for one of the stones as I said, "I don't know about you, but they look like emeralds to me."

Jake grabbed my arm before I could retrieve one. "Hang on a second." Taking an evidence bag from his pocket, my husband handed it to me. "Use the bag to pick each one up individually so you don't mess with the fingerprints." After pulling out another bag, he said, "Transfer them into this as you go."

"How many of these things do you carry around with you?" I asked him.

"More than enough for the task at hand," he replied. "Besides, you can put more than one in each bag if you want to."

By the time the wall cavity was empty, there were seven emeralds of differing sizes and weights in the evidence baggie. I looked at them in the light before handing them to Jake. "What do you think?"

"I think you won't have to get a loan to pay for your renovations now."

"What do you mean?"

"Suzanne, you own the building free and clear, and my guess is that includes whatever was inside when you bought it. These are yours, as far as I'm concerned."

The thought of it shocked me. "Are you telling me that someone stashed these away in the walls legitimately?"

"How do you think they got there?" he asked me.

I grabbed one of the newspapers. "I don't know, but I have a sneaky suspicion that my stepfather might have an idea. Let's call him and have him come over."

Phillip and Momma made it to the donut shop in seven minutes. I may have made it sound a little more urgent than it really was on the phone, but having what could be very valuable gems on hand made me a little nervous. I knew a lot of their worth depended on several different factors, but they all looked precious to me.

"What have you got there?" Phillip asked as he tucked a spiral notebook under one arm after walking inside.

Jake handed him the stones, and after a perfunctory glance at them, he handed the baggie to Momma. "I'm talking about the newspapers." Phillip loved to research old crimes that had occurred in the area, so when I saw so many old newspapers, including the one I'd stepped over when I'd found Snappy's body, I knew he was the one to call. Sure, we'd let Chief Grant know what was going on as well, but for the moment, that was yet to be determined, at least as far as I was concerned. After studying a few of the newspaper dates and headlines, Phillip frowned a moment before he spoke. "Unless I miss my guess, those are the Hathaway jewels, or at least some of them."

"What are you talking about?" I asked him.

Phillip leafed through his notebook before settling on a particular section. "In 1922, Amelia Hathaway's home was robbed. Her father was a jeweler from New York who was traveling to see his daughter on his way to Atlanta with a large inventory of emeralds. Apparently Cornwall Hathaway liked to show off the jewels to staff and friends of his daughter's to show how wealthy he really was. She didn't have a safe, so in the middle of the night, someone broke into Cornwall's room, knocked him on the head with a lamp base, and stole the jewels. They never found the thief, or the gems, either, for that matter. Let's see, there were fifteen emeralds taken altogether, so unless I miss my guess, Snappy found the other eight in the cavity next to the one where you found these, and someone killed him for them."

"Hold on a second," Jake said. "That's all supposition, and you know it."

"Not all of it. Chief Grant called me ten minutes before you did," Phillip said. "He asked if I thought it was significant that an old newspaper with blood on it was found at the scene. He knows my penchant for history, and I was just digging into where it could have come from when you called." The retired chief pulled out his small spiral notebook and glanced through a few entries. "The date of the robbery matches the newspapers, so is it that farfetched to believe that Snappy found the first half batch of stones and was murdered before he could uncover these?"

"You know what we need to do," Jake said with a grim expression.

"Call Chief Grant?" I asked.

"True, but it's not time to do that just yet. Suzanne, how do you feel about a little more impromptu remodeling?"

That's when I got it. "We need to pull the rest of the plaster from the walls to make sure there's nothing else there."

"I'm truly sorry about that."

"It's okay," I said. "As you told me earlier, at least I'll be able to pay for the remodeling now."

"We'll have to wait to see about that, I'm afraid," Momma said.

"What do you mean?"

"There are still Hathaways in town," she said softly.

"And if these stones belong to them, they can't belong to me."

"Not necessarily," Jake said. "The insurance company had to have paid for the loss. Technically, the jewels could still belong to whoever insured the old man."

"Let's not get ahead of ourselves," I said. "No matter who's paying, the plaster in here still needs to come off the walls."

"Would you like me to do it?" Jake asked gently.

"Thanks, but no. I seem to have a knack for it."

In short order, there was no more plaster on any of the walls out front.

I took no solace in the fact that we hadn't made any more discoveries.

Evidently we'd cleared the last cache there had been.

Now the question was what were we going to do about our discovery?

"Does anyone have any idea how we can use these stones to our advantage?" Jake asked as we finished picking up the plaster remnants, bagging them, and dumping them out in back of the shop. Snappy had rented a dumpster for demolition, but he'd opted for the smallest version available, and it was getting perilously full.

"You make them sound so common, but they can be quite rare," Momma said. "I've loved emeralds for years. Did you realize that some of the finest in the world have been found right here in North Carolina?"

"I'm guessing that these weren't, though," Jake said. "I fully realize that we need to tell the chief of police about these, but the question is, when do we make the call?" he asked after a moment's thought.

"Immediately," Phillip said firmly. "He probably doesn't have any idea what the real motive in Snappy's murder was."

"We don't know that for sure ourselves yet," Jake reminded him.

Phillip countered, "If Snappy wasn't killed for the emeralds, then where exactly are the other stones? They obviously aren't here, and there were sections of the newspaper from the same time period in both cavities, the one we found, and Snappy's original discovery. Those emeralds are out there somewhere. If nothing else, their absence here demands it."

"That's assuming the entire lot was stashed here originally," I said.

"You don't think someone hid these recently, do you?" Momma asked me.

"No, that plaster was far too old for that to be possible. What if there were two thieves, though, and only one hid his share here? Or what if there was a single thief, and he split them up, hiding them in different places?"

"It still doesn't explain the newspaper you saw on the floor when you found Snappy's body," Jake said. "We know for a fact it didn't come from the hiding place we found tonight."

Phillip stared off into space for a few moments before he spoke again. "It's safer to assume that the entire hoard was stashed here, and I may know the answer as to why."

"Have you been holding out on us, Phillip?" Jake asked the retired chief of police. His voice was light and airy, but there was a hint of steel in it as well.

"No, not at all. I just realized something, that's all."

"Well, don't keep it to yourself, dear," Momma told her husband. "Share it with the rest of the class."

"Repairs were made on this structure around the time of

the robbery when this place was still an active train depot and not a donut shop," Phillip explained. "I wasn't looking for the information, but in one of the articles in the archives about the theft, there was mention of a contractor working here during that time."

I knew my building had a wonderful history of serving the residents of April Springs, but it was nice to be reminded of it. "Do you have any idea who the contractor was?"

"Henry Chastain," he said after consulting his notes.

"You thought that was important enough to write down?" Momma asked him.

Phillip reddened slightly. "I thought Suzanne might find it interesting, that's all."

"I do," I said. "Thank you for thinking of me."

"Happy to," he answered, clearly uncomfortable about the attention.

"Getting back to the case," Jake said, reminding us all of what we were talking about. "How is that significant?"

"Chastain had a daughter named Bess who worked as the upstairs maid at the Hathaway home," Phillip said. "There was some speculation when she disappeared shortly after the theft, but most folks figured she'd just run off with Barton Grass. Only Barton came back through town years later and claimed that he'd last seen Bess the day before she'd disappeared, and he just assumed there had been someone else in her life."

"So, the girl disappears about the same time as the theft," Jake said, and I could almost see the wheels churning in his mind. "If she'd absconded with the stones, that would be one thing, but why hide them here and then disappear?"

"What if she never went anywhere?" Phillip asked gravely. "Fifteen years ago, they had to drain the quarry for an expansion project, and they found the skeletal remains of a woman in her late teens or early twenties. There was a pendant around her neck with a large C on it, and some folks thought it might be the missing Chastain girl."

"So, she stole the gems after conking Hathaway on the noggin, took them here in the dead of night and hid them behind the walls her father was fixing the next day. What happened to her after that? And if those were her bones in the quarry, did someone kill her, or did she drown herself out of remorse for what she'd done?" I asked.

"I'm not sure we'll ever know the answer to those questions," Jake said as he stood beside one of the walls that had been demolished before I'd gotten started myself. Shining a much bigger flashlight into the opening than I'd had, he took out another baggie, reached down, and worked something loose that had shone in the light.

"Well, will you look at that? I just found another emerald," he said in surprise. "Evidently both batches were originally hidden here after all."

"Where did you find that?" I asked as I joined him. "I checked that wall myself."

"It wasn't easy to spot," Jake said. "It had fallen down and wedged itself between two floorboards. I'm guessing Snappy missed it, and so did his killer. I doubt the police had much call to search it so thoroughly without knowing about the emeralds hidden there."

"So, both sets of jewels were here until they were unearthed recently," Momma said. "We need to check the local pawnshops and jewelry stores."

I doubted my mother had ever been in a pawnshop in her life, though I knew she'd visited more than one jeweler in her day. "That's a leap, isn't it?" I asked her.

"Hear me out. The jewelry-store angle might not make sense after all. There could be some embarrassing questions that the killer wouldn't be able to answer. No, the pawnshop would be the better choice," Momma said. "Suzanne, let's say you killed Snappy."

I interrupted her. "If it's all the same to you, I'd rather we didn't."

"Fine. We'll call the killer X for convenience's sake. X comes to the donut shop to see Snappy. Maybe one of his potential heirs found out they weren't getting what they'd been promised. The killer catches Snappy with the stolen gems and decides to get what's rightfully coming to them, at least in their minds. They stab him with the screwdriver and grab the stones. Only they're in a hurry, and for some reason, they can't hang around much longer to search for any more that might have been hidden here. They scoop up the stones they can see, and then they leave as quickly as they can. Only there's a problem. Greed sets in. What if there are more stones hidden than Snappy found? It's a natural enough thing to wonder. Soon, it's all the killer can think about, the possibility that there are more, even better jewels, still hidden here. It makes sense that the killer would come back to Donut Hearts to see what they might have missed after everyone has gone home for the night."

The premise gave me chills. "Are you saying whoever killed Snappy is coming back tonight?"

"It's entirely possible," Momma said. "Anyway, it's all just idle speculation at this point, but it might be worth sticking around in order to find out one way or the other."

I looked over to see Jake and Phillip looking at my mother in awe. "You know, you might just be right, Dorothea," Jake said, and then he turned to Momma's husband. "What do you say, Phillip? Do you feel like going out on a stakeout with me here tonight?"

"Shouldn't we just turn this over to Chief Grant and be done with it?" I asked.

Jake frowned for a moment before answering. "He's spread

thin as it is, and we don't have much in the way of hard evidence to go on as things stand. What could it hurt to wait and bring him up to speed in the morning?"

"No hard evidence other than the emeralds, you mean?" I asked him with a grin.

"Sure, other than that. Don't forget, Phillip and I are both perfectly capable of handling things here on the off chance the killer does decide to come back, and if they don't show, we haven't wasted any of the police chief's valuable time. What do you say? Wouldn't you love to know who did this, Suzanne?"

"I would," I admitted. "Momma, what do you think?"

Phillip looked at her with open anticipation, and I had a feeling that she found she couldn't bring herself to say no to him. "Fine, but I'm setting a few conditions before I agree to anything."

"Whatever you say," Phillip said.

"Hang on a second. What did you have in mind, Dorothea?" Jake asked my mother.

"No worries, it shouldn't be too arduous for either one of you. If you hear someone outside trying to break in, or if you suspect something is about to happen, you are to call the chief and tell him what you're doing, and I mean immediately. Do not, under any circumstances, try to handle this without him. Have I made myself understood?"

Both men nodded as though they were a pair of scolded schoolchildren, and I could see that it was all Momma could do not to laugh out loud at them. I myself was biting my lower lip in an effort not to let my mirth explode.

"Very well. If you two are going to stay here on your stakeout, these gems are going directly into my safe at home."

"What if we need a few of them for bait later?" Jake asked.

"I've got something that should do nicely in their place, but we're not risking these," Momma said.

Jake frowned, clearly unhappy about this latest development. "No offense, Dot, but there are a great many crooks who will know a fake from a mile away."

"What makes you think I have any fakes?" Momma asked him with a grin.

"You're just full of surprises, aren't you?" Jake asked her, smiling in kind.

"I have my moments. As for visiting the pawnshops in the area, where else would an amateur unload several emeralds in a hurry if the jewelry stores would be unavailable to them? Surely they don't want to be caught red-handed with the emeralds. If tonight yields no results, we need to get Chief Grant's approval to start visiting pawnshops in the area and see if anyone's been trying to unload some cut emeralds that haven't been set yet." She turned to her husband as she added, "Now, Phillip, you'll need some provisions for this little adventure you're going to have tonight. Would you like to stay here with Jake while I fetch them, or would you care to come with me?" The man looked absolutely traumatized by the prospect of leaving the donut shop, so Momma quickly added, "Never mind. Suzanne, would you care to join me?"

"You bet I would," I said as I paused to kiss my husband good-bye, at least for the moment, and walked out of the shop with my mother.

CHAPTER 9

B Y THE TIME WE GOT back to the donut shop with supplies, the men were settled in. Jake had even made coffee, something I'd neglected to do. "I'm glad to see that you men can take care of yourselves," I said as I handed them both sandwiches for later.

"Don't be *too* confident in our abilities," Jake said with a smile. "What else do you have in that bag?"

"There are all kinds of goodies," Momma said. "What have you two been up to since we've been gone?"

"We decided that the best place to wait for any unwelcome visitors is behind the counter," Phillip said. "By the way, where did you get those moving blankets in back, Suzanne?"

"One of my out-of-town customers lost his wallet last week, so we bartered for donuts," I said. "I don't normally do that, but he comes by every month, and he's a really nice guy. He makes some of the blankets that movers use, and that was all he had in his truck. I still might not have done it, but he had his little boy with him, and there was no way I was going to say no to that sweet little face. I offered to float him the donuts on credit, but he wouldn't hear of it, thus the blankets. I'm glad you're putting them to good use."

"I think you got the better part of the deal," Jake said. "Not that your donuts aren't worth every penny, but exactly how many donuts did you trade for?" When I didn't say anything,

Jake raised an eyebrow, showing that he was still waiting for my answer. I wasn't going to be able to duck this one.

"Okay, so I gave him two twenties so he could buy enough gas to get back home, as well," I said. "Nobody here had better judge me. If you'd been in my shoes, you'd have done the exact same thing."

Momma walked over and, without a word, hugged me fiercely. "I'm proud of you, Suzanne."

"I hope so, but this was just the right thing to do. *Anybody* would have done it in my place."

"Would that it were true," Momma said, and then she looked at our husbands. "I've been giving this some thought, and I truly believe that you should inform the chief of police about what's going on before you conduct your stakeout tonight." Before either man could speak, Momma raised a hand in the air to keep them silent, and they clearly knew better than to challenge her. "I fully realize that you are both immensely overqualified to do this on your own, but do I really need to remind you that neither of you are still active in law enforcement? Besides, isn't there such a thing as professional courtesy? How is Stephen Grant going to feel when he hears about this?"

Momma was clearly going to go on, but she was interrupted by a knock at the door. Chief Grant himself walked in after I let him in, and he was carrying three sleeping bags with him to boot. "Sorry I'm late," he said with a grin.

"Did you two call him?" Momma asked the men sternly.

"We came to the same conclusion you did earlier," Phillip said with a smile.

"Then why on earth did you let me go on lecturing you?" she asked them.

Jake laughed. "I don't know about your husband, but there was no way that I was going to interrupt you when you were on a roll like that."

Momma looked at me. "Men."

"I quit trying to figure them out years ago, and I'm much happier these days," I told her.

"Sorry, dear," Phillip said. "We should have led with that."

"No worries," my mother said as she patted his cheek affectionately. She then turned to the police chief. "Does your presence mean that you approve of this impromptu stakeout?"

"The emeralds may just help me solve this murder case, so I'm not exactly in any position to be picky at this point. Besides, if the killer *does* come back, we might have this thing wrapped up by midnight. The worst thing that can happen is that I get to spend a few hours with two of my predecessors, and I'm not foolish enough to pass up an opportunity to learn more from them."

"You're further along than you give yourself credit for," Jake said.

"I agree completely," Phillip added.

"Thanks. I appreciate that more than I can say." The chief looked at us in turn, and then he said, "Ladies, I hate to kill this party, but there's no way anybody's going to try to break in if it looks like we're having a bash in here."

"You're right," I said as I stifled a yawn. "Besides, if I'm going to be making donuts soon, I'd better get at least a little sleep. Are you coming, Momma?"

"I'm right behind you," she replied. "Now you gentlemen be careful, do you understand me?"

"Don't worry about us. If someone tries to get in here, they won't stand a chance," Phillip said with a grin. It was clear he was having the time of his life.

"Just don't do anything foolish," Momma replied.

"If you're going to handcuff me like that, then I might as well come home with you," he said, still grinning, though it was clear he didn't mean one word of it.

Out on the sidewalk, I pulled my coat closer and told my mother, "You're welcome to come back to the cottage with me if you'd like."

"Thanks, but you need your rest, and I've got some contracts I need to go over before morning. If you need me, don't hesitate to call."

"Right back at you. I love you, Momma."

"And I, you," she said with a gentle smile I knew so well.

I headed back to the cottage driving Jake's truck, since there didn't need to be any indication that the donut shop was now being occupied by three proficient lawmen, even if two of them were retired. I flipped on the lights inside my home, added another log to the fire, and then I crept off to bed.

I couldn't sleep, though.

I'm usually quite thankful for my imagination, but tonight, it was giving me fits, coming up with a dozen different scenarios that all ended badly for three men I cared so much about. I got out of bed, walked out into the living room, and curled up on the couch to watch the fire, hoping it might help ease my mind somehow.

In less than a minute, I was sound asleep. There was something about a cold winter wind outside and a fire crackling inside that always seemed to knock me out.

It was a good thing I'd set the alarm on my cell phone. Otherwise, I might have slept for another hour or two past my time to get up. As it was, I woke up and had to get ready in a rush to make it to the donut shop in time, all the time wondering if anything had happened the night before, even though I realized that I would find out soon enough.

I went outside and tried to crank up the Jeep, but the cold must have killed the last of the life left in my battery, because it wouldn't start. I'd have to get Jake to replace it while I was at work, but there was no way I was going to walk through the park in the dark during the first part of January, especially with the possibility of a killer lurking somewhere in the shadows. Fortunately Jake's truck started up on the first try, and as I drove the short distance to work, I wondered what I'd find at Donut Hearts. I parked in my usual space, but it suddenly occurred to me that it might not be the smartest thing in the world to do to walk into a dark building where three armed men were waiting.

I pulled out my phone and dialed Jake's number.

"I'm here," I said.

"I know. I watched you drive up," he said as he stepped outside through the unlocked door.

"Wow, I need this kind of service every morning," I said as I walked into the shop. The lights in the kitchen were on, but I flipped the ones out front on as well.

The three men shielded their eyes, and I reached for the switch immediately. "Sorry about that," I apologized as my mother came out from the kitchen. "Momma, what are you doing here?"

"I couldn't sleep," she confessed. "Don't worry, I didn't jeopardize the stakeout. I just got here myself."

"I take it you didn't have any luck," I said as I walked into the kitchen and turned the fryer on, always the first order of business of any donut-making day.

"Well, we shared a few good stories while we waited, and we decided a few things as well," Jake said with a shrug. "It was a long shot, anyway, but we at least had to try."

"Sorry you didn't catch any bad guys," I said as I patted his shoulder.

"No worries. At least we managed to come up with a plan while we were waiting," Phillip answered. "The chief is going to go ahead and check out all of the area pawnshops this morning, and then the four of us are going to do the same thing this afternoon after you close Donut Hearts for the day."

"Why are we all doing the same thing after you if you're already going around asking the questions first?" I asked Chief Grant curiously.

The chief replied, "Sometimes the answer to an official question isn't the same as one asked off the record by civilians who are in the buying mood."

"If nobody admits to getting an inquiry, we're going to show each pawnshop a few emeralds ourselves as proof of our sincerity," Jake said with a grin. "That should bring out their greed if civic duty isn't enough."

"That's the sticking point we were going over just before Dorothea arrived," the chief of police said. "I don't want these emeralds leaving my sight until we resolve this mess one way or the other."

"They may not have to," Momma said softly.

"I don't see how."

"What if each team had two emeralds apiece, purely for show?" she asked him. "Do you think that would be enough bait?"

"I just said I don't feel comfortable using these as lures to unmask a killer," Chief Grant said as he held the bag up in front of him.

"And fakes won't work," Jake added. "We discussed that already, too."

"We won't use fakes, and those aren't the *only* emeralds in North Carolina, you know," Momma said.

"I understand that, but where are you going to get substitutes on such short notice?"

"All I need to do is go by one of my safety deposit boxes when the bank opens, and then we'll be set," my mother answered.

"Are you telling me that you have loose emeralds just lying around somewhere?" Phillip asked his wife, clearly surprised by the latest twist.

"I wouldn't say they were just lying around, but yes, I happen to have four stones that will do as substitutes for the ones found earlier. I'm sorry I didn't mention having them before."

Phillip grinned at his wife. "Dorothea, I didn't marry you for your money or your jewels. I love *you*."

"And I love you, too," she said with a smile, "but it doesn't hurt that I'm rich, does it?"

Phillip just shook his head and laughed. "I'll take you any way I can get you, for richer or for poorer, in sickness and in health."

"So, it's settled," Momma said. "We take two teams out to canvass local pawnshops in the afternoon after the chief has had his crack at them first."

"And you're okay with this?" I asked Chief Grant.

"Officially, I don't have an opinion one way or the other."

"How about unofficially?" I followed up.

"What could it hurt?" He smiled at me on his way out. "As long as we don't use the emeralds you found here in the shop, I'm good with the plan. Thanks for the coffee, Suzanne. Gentlemen, it was a real pleasure."

"For us, as well," Phillip said. "We'd better be going, too, Dorothea."

"We'll see you later today, Suzanne," Momma said as she ducked out along with her husband.

After they were gone, Jake said, "It was nice of you to bring my truck by."

"Actually, the Jeep battery died," I confessed. "Is there any chance you can get it fixed for me while I'm at work this morning?"

"Fixed? No. Replaced? You bet." Jake looked around the shop. "Do you need me to hang around and help out?"

It was obvious the request wasn't sincere, and I had half a mind to take him up on it just to see what he'd say, but he was sleep deprived as it was, so I saw no need to pile on. "Go home and get some rest. I'll see you a little after eleven, and we can start hitting pawnshops together."

"That sounds like a plan to me," Jake said. "Who knows? Maybe one of us will get lucky."

"As far as I'm concerned, I already did," I said as I kissed him good-bye.

"I meant in the investigation."

"So, you don't agree with me?" I asked him, laughing.

"Oh, no. We both got lucky. There's no doubt about that. I'll see you later. Happy donut making."

"Thanks."

After Jake was gone, I took the cups they'd drunk from and put them in the sink in the kitchen. After that, I emptied the last of the coffee and started a fresh batch, as was my habit. It was time to get things back to normal and get into my daily routine. The men might not have captured the killer, but I still had a job to do.

April Springs was going to be expecting donuts in three hours, so I'd better get busy making them.

"Wow, this place is a real mess! I can't believe someone was murdered here yesterday," Emma said as she walked in an hour after I'd arrived.

"It's tragic, isn't it?"

"It surely is. In fact, there's only one good thing about the first of the year as far as I'm concerned."

"What's that?" I asked her, curious about her statement.

"No more pumpkin donuts!" Emma said with enthusiasm.

"I thought you liked them."

"To eat, yes. To clean up after, no thank you. I'm perfectly happy seeing them gone for another year."

I'd already made a nice selection of cake donuts before she'd arrived, but pumpkin donuts were now officially off the menu until October first. I could have probably sold them year round, but I liked having certain seasonal treats for sale at Donut Hearts. For example, come May when the local strawberries were harvested, I'd offer strawberry shortcake donuts, and in September, I made a special apple cinnamon cake donut with apple cider icing that was one of my own personal favorites. Unfortunately, January brought us snowball donuts, one of my least favorite personal selections. It was really nothing more than a plain cake donut dipped in icing first and then smothered in shredded coconut. I wouldn't eat one on a dare, but some of my customers adored them. "That's fine, but now you have to deal with shredded coconut everywhere," I warned her.

"We all have our own personal trials and tribulations," Emma said with a shrug, and I hoped she was just kidding. In the scale of world problems, donuts shouldn't have even made the top one thousand list.

"What's your dad think about the murder happening here?" I asked her as I prepped the yeast donuts by mixing the ingredients in my massive floor mixer. The sound of the motor was loud, but we'd grown used to it over the years, and now it was second nature talking over the drone of the machine.

"He thinks someone's going after contractors," Emma said. "Did you hear about the plumber who drowned in Lenoir last week?"

"The way I heard it, he was kayaking on the Catawba River," I said, "and now they're saying he had a heart attack in the cold weather and tipped over and drowned. He wasn't even wearing a life jacket."

"You know my father. He has his own unique way of looking

at things," Emma said. Truer words had never been spoken. "What do you think about Snappy's murder, Suzanne? Do you think someone local did it?"

I wasn't about to tell Emma about the emeralds we'd found last night, but I decided to hold onto that particular piece of information. "I suppose it's possible," I told her, knowing that it was the farthest thing from the truth, at least in my opinion.

"Are you and Jake digging into it?" Emma asked me, and then she quickly countered with, "Strike that."

I just smiled at her. "Consider it stricken." We'd worked out an arrangement in the past where I didn't tell Emma anything I didn't want her dad to hear and possibly print. "It's almost time for our break. It's not too cold out for you, is it?"

"I think it's going to be refreshing," she replied with a grin.

"Okay, if you say so," I answered.

Once the dough was ready to be left alone, I set my timer, and we walked outside. My customers were back to making do with folding chairs since the construction had started, since there was no way on earth I was going to leave the nice new things my book-club friends had given me during our remodeling and repairs. We grabbed a pair of folding chairs and walked outside together.

"Do you know what we really need?" Emma asked me as she rubbed her hands together.

"A trip to the Bahamas?" I asked her.

She laughed. "I mean besides that. If there's any room in the budget after the remodel, we should get one of those portable propane heaters out here for our breaks in the cold weather."

"Emma, we'll be lucky to be able to afford a pack of matches after everything's finished, but I'll keep it in mind."

At that moment, a car drove past us slowly, one I didn't recognize. When they realized Emma and I were sitting out front watching them, the driver hurried down the road toward my cottage. "What's up with that?" Emma asked me. "Grace is still out of town, so it can't be for her. Is it possible it's a friend of Jake's?"

"I don't think so. Not at this time of night, anyway. Let's give it a second and see if they turn around and come back."

Sure enough, two minutes later, the sedan whizzed back past us, going much too fast for Springs Drive day or night. The windows were tinted, and I couldn't get a good look at who might be inside, so I got my phone out to take a picture of the license plate.

Whoever had been driving had put a paper bag over it, obscuring the letters and numbers completely.

"That was odd," Emma said after the car was gone.

"Agreed," I answered. Had someone been out cruising April Springs a little after four in the morning by coincidence, or had they come to see if Donut Hearts was empty? If it had been innocent, then why had the license plate number been so artfully obscured? "Did you catch the make or model of that car, by any chance?"

"It was blue, I think. Maybe black. I suppose it could have even been dark red. It was honestly too dark to see. We need another streetlight out here, don't we?"

"I'll talk to the mayor, but I think his budget is even tighter than ours," I replied. I wished I'd snapped a photo of the car anyway while I'd had the chance, but I'd been so thrown by the bag that I'd forgotten to. I wasn't very good with car models either, and I wasn't entirely sure if I could have identified the strange car in the daylight. My timer chose that moment to go off, so I stood, grabbing my chair and folding it before we went inside.

"If they want donuts, they're just going to have to come back when we're open," Emma said with a grin.

"Do you think they were on a treat run?" I asked her.

"Why not? What else could it be?"

I wasn't about to tell her that it might be the killer returning to the scene of the crime to search for more emeralds. That was all I needed, to have Ray Blake mucking about in our investigation. Was that how the police chief felt about my cohorts and me? Probably, but there wasn't much I could do about it. I'd mention it to Jake later, but for now, it was once again time to make new treats.

CHAPTER 10

MY NEW CONTRACTOR DIDN'T EVEN have to wait for me to open the front door a little before five a.m. "You must be Mr. Young. Sorry, but I didn't get your first name," I said as I offered him my hand.

"Just Young is fine," he said gruffly. He was clearly not used to being up at this hour of the day, though I was just hitting my stride. I had fifteen minutes of free time before the yeast donuts started going into the oil, so it was the perfect time for me to show him around.

"Okay," I said, thinking it odd to call the man by his last name only. "You can see what you're dealing with."

He looked at the plasterless walls in the front and nodded his approval. "This looks good. As a matter of fact, it's better than I was expecting. This is going to save us from patching things up and trying to make the new and the old match. We can do it, but it takes more time and costs more as well. Do you want plaster again?"

"Actually, I thought shiplap boards painted white and antiqued in spots would be nice," I said. "I've cut a picture from a magazine to show you what I had in mind." I'd been perusing home-improvement magazines for days looking for something I liked, and I'd come across the horizontally mounted decorative wide boards in one. In some ways, it matched the building better than the original plaster had. "Can you do that?"

"Sure. It'll be cheaper, too. How about the outside?"

"I'd like that to match the old work if it's at all possible."

"I don't see why not," he said as he jotted a few things down onto his clipboard.

"Do you want to keep the picture?" I asked.

"No thanks. I don't need it." After a few more moments, he asked, "What about the floor? Do you want that to be the same?" He kicked at a few spots where the falling tree had gouged out a few chunks. "Are we just doing a patch and paint here?"

"I would like it patched, and there are a few places that need to be leveled, but instead of plum, I'd like a mottled gray instead."

"Got it. Battleship-gray floor," he said as he wrote it down.

"No. Mottled, like weathered barn board," I repeated, not sure that he was getting my vision at all. "If you don't mind, I'd like a sample of the wall and the floor finishes before you do anything else to make sure we're on the right page."

He looked at me as though he was massively annoyed with me, but I didn't care. I'd be looking at the donut shop's interior for years to come, and I wanted it to be right. A deep, lustrous weathered gray with layered highlights on the floor would be soothing. Battleship gray would remind me of my elementary school cafeteria. Granted, it might be a fine line, but I wanted to make sure he abided by it. He frowned at me a moment before saying, "Most of the job should be fairly straightforward, but the floor is going to be the real problem."

"What do you mean?" I asked. "Can't you just repaint it a different color?"

He shook his head curtly. "I wish it were that easy. The concrete will have to be patched, leveled in a few spots, sanded, washed, and dried thoroughly. Then you're going to need two coats of stain, and then two of sealer. All in all, it will take me about a week, and that's rushing it."

"A week! I can't afford to close for a week. What about a wood floor instead?" I'd toyed with the idea earlier, especially every time I went into the hardware store and saw those old, scarred pine floorboards they had there.

Young scratched his chin for a moment, and then he said, "The wood planks take two days to acclimate, and while that's happening, we need to put down a moisture barrier, a new subfloor with sleepers, and plywood before we do any installation. You're looking at three to four days for that."

It was still too long. "Is there anything you can do so I don't have to shut Donut Hearts down at all?"

The contractor got down on one knee and looked at the floor again. "They've got something new you might like. We can patch the gouges, level a few of the worst spots of the floor, and then put down floating vinyl floor right on top of it, given that amount of time."

I didn't want an ugly floor in my beautiful shop. "I'm not sure I'd be happy with that."

"You don't have to make up your mind right now," he said. "I'll bring you some samples. You might be surprised by what's out there these days."

"Fine, but I still need to approve it first," I said, though I wasn't entirely convinced vinyl was a viable option. Still, it might be the best I could do given my time constraints. Besides, if I hated it, I could always have it ripped out and start over, so I couldn't afford to just dismiss it out of hand, at least not until I'd seen some samples first.

"Is there anything else?" he asked me.

"Just one more thing. When can you get started?" I questioned him.

"This afternoon," Young said.

"Really? So soon?"

"If that's a problem, we can push it if you're not ready for us," Young said with a frown. "Your mother said this was a priority, so I just assumed you'd like it sooner rather than later."

"This afternoon would be great," I said. "Do I need to be here when you're working?" Jake and I had a date to visit the pawnshops in Maple Hollow, but if I had to push them for my remodel, we could always delay our trip until I'd consulted with the contractor.

"No, we can do the work without you." He studied his clipboard then nodded. "I'll bring samples of the shiplap and some floor choices by around ten. If you approve of the selections, we'll get started after you're closed for the day."

"Excellent. Would you like a cake donut and some coffee while you're here?"

"No offense, but I never cared for donuts, and I don't drink coffee."

"Then I guess we're done here," I said as I showed him out. I didn't trust people who didn't like donuts, but I was willing to make an exception this time. I was getting truly tired of living with the temporary fixes my friends had been so kind to make.

Young paused at the door and looked around one last time. "Snappy shouldn't have destroyed all of your walls, even if it does make my job easier. It's clear from the walls and the ceiling that the damage was only in one section, but that was the way the man operated. Why charge you for a nickel if he could stretch it to a dime?"

"Did you know him all that well?" I asked.

"Not really," Young said. "We didn't get along. It's still a shame that he's dead."

"You won't have any problem working in the space where he was murdered, will you?" I asked him.

"No, not one bit."

I just hoped that he was a better contractor than he was a person.

"Good morning, Suzanne. I'd like a dozen donuts, please. Feel free to choose any you'd like for my selection."

It was a little after seven, and I was surprised to see one of my suspects, Deloris Mack, in my donut shop ordering my treats so recently after her ex-husband had been murdered there.

"Are you okay being here?" I asked her as I did as she asked.

Deloris looked around the space, seeming to take it all in. "I had no choice. I needed to see where it happened for my own peace of mind. Where exactly did you find him?"

I pointed to the spot where Snappy's body had been. She gravely took a few steps and stood over it, staring down at the floor at her feet. Running her hands through the air as she wiggled her fingers, it looked as though she were trying to absorb the karma of the crime scene. Either that or playing an imaginary piano. I'd known the day before from her attire that the older woman had a New Age feel to her, and her current behavior did nothing to change my mind. After a few more moments of movement, she seemed to gather the air around her to her chest, and then finally, she shoved it all away from her as she nodded her head once in dismissal. "I'm so glad I came. He's at peace now."

"How can you be so sure?" I asked her, honestly curious about such a statement.

"Do you doubt me?" Deloris asked as she glanced furtively around at the exposed wood and bricks of the walls. Was she hoping to find more emeralds hiding there, or was it simply an innocent gesture? I was getting awfully paranoid, and I knew that I had to stop it if I was going to keep conducting my investigation, even though sometimes a little paranoia was a good thing. After all, it had saved my life on more than one occasion.

"No, of course not. I'm the first to admit that there are more things going on in this world than I'll ever be aware of."

"How very enlightened of you," Deloris said in response, clearly pleased by my answer.

I was handing her change to her when Hank Bloch walked in.

They looked surprised to see each other, but they both recovered quickly. "Deloris, you're a little far away from your candle shop, aren't you? Did you come by to offer some kind of voodoo hooey to tame the bad juju in the place?" It was immediately clear that the two weren't big fans of each other.

"Thank goodness not everyone is as Neanderthal about my beliefs as you are." She scowled at him for a moment before asking, "I'm surprised you were able to find your way out of Maple Hollow. What brings you here?"

"I started to feel bad about not finishing this job for Suzanne," Hank said. "After all, Snappy took this on, and we were partners through thick and thin." He whistled softly as he checked out our walls. "I hadn't realized he was doing a full demolition in here. It's going to take more work than I was expecting." Was that a look of disappointment on his face as he noticed that all of the studs were now exposed? Funny, but Young had been elated that he wouldn't have to match old plaster. Perhaps they were motivated by different intentions.

"It is what it is," I said as noncommittally as I could manage.

"Well, I can't get to you this week, but I can make time next week for sure, three at the outside."

"Thanks, but I've already found someone else," I told him.

He looked surprised. "That was quick."

"What can I say? It needs to be done." I wasn't about to tell him that my mother had expedited the process.

"Okay, if you're sure," he said. "I just wanted to check in and see if I could lend a hand here, but if you've got it covered, I'm going back to my other job."

"Ripping off widows and children, I presume?" Deloris asked him.

"Are you still here?" Bloch asked her, trying his best to act surprised, though she'd clearly been standing there the entire time. "You know, when a woman like you reaches a certain age, she starts to become invisible to most men."

I could see that Deloris was firing up a response, and I knew that I needed to step in. "Thanks for coming by, both of you. Deloris, enjoy those donuts. Mr. Bloch, thank you for your concern. I hope you both have better days today than you each did yesterday."

That seemed to take the wind out of their sails, and they both left grumpily. I didn't care if they resumed their argument outside, though I would have preferred it not being in front of Donut Hearts, but it was still better than having to hear it inside myself.

"What was that all about?" Emma asked as she poked her head out of the kitchen after they were gone.

"Just two customers who couldn't get along with each other," I said, not really answering her question. I wasn't about to tell her and, by proxy, perhaps her father, that two of my prime suspects had just made it a point to examine the interior of my donut shop, regardless of what their stated reasons might have been.

I was wondering if we'd see Snappy's son or his girlfriend anytime soon when the front door opened later, and to my delight, Young walked in with batches of things under his arms. Glancing at the clock on the wall, I saw that it was two minutes until ten.

He'd kept his word so far, which was a very good sign indeed.

"I got those samples like I promised," the man said as he laid his pile of things on the display counter. I would have rather he'd used a table, but in his defense, we were still getting by with folding chairs only, so there were none in sight.

"Let's see what you've been able to come up with," I said.

He pulled out two small sections of shiplap boards, both painted white and antiqued exactly like they'd been in my picture. "They fit together like this," he said as he butted the two long edges together. He'd randomly sanded the boards after they'd been painted, and he held them against the wall to show me the full effect.

I marveled at just how good they looked there and knew instantly that it had been the right choice.

"Perfect. If the rest of the boards look this good, we'll be in great shape."

"They will," he said. Was that the hint of a grin on his face upon receiving my approval? Next, he took a sample of gray, nondescript vinyl flooring and laid it on the concrete.

"I hate it," I said, ready to dismiss the idea entirely.

"Hang on. I've got more options," he protested.

"Fine, but I can tell you now, they aren't going to work."

Young pulled another long, thin sheet from the stack and replaced the earlier one. It featured a weathered gray wood-grain print, and from where I was standing, it was difficult to tell that it wasn't the real thing.

I knew in an instant that this was the floor I needed for Donut Hearts. "That's perfect. How do the seams look?"

"You'll never see them unless you get down on your hands and knees," he said. "They snap together like some kind of kid's hobby kit, they're tough, and they'll float on the concrete subfloor like a dream. We won't even have to prime the concrete after we get it all leveled out with quick-drying cement."

"Sold."

"Good. That's all I'll need then, except a key to the place."

I was reluctant to hand over a key to Donut Hearts to anyone, particularly someone I didn't really know, and he must have seen something in my expression. "Listen, if you're uncomfortable giving me one, that's fine. If you want to stay here while we work, it won't be a problem. You won't be able to get in our way, though. Otherwise, you need to let me have a key. Don't worry. You can trust me."

"I can't tell you how many times I've heard that before, usually to my regret," I said with a wry smile.

"You've never heard it from me, though. It's your call, though."

I was being silly, and I knew it. I walked over to the register, hit No Sale, and retrieved our spare key from the drawer. "Here you go."

"Thanks," he said as he pocketed it and collected his samples. "I'll take good care of it." As he gathered up his samples, he grinned at me as he said, "I'll be back."

"I'm looking forward to it," I said, and then he was gone. The interior walls were going to be perfect, and I had a hunch the floor would be fine, too. Vinyl wasn't as durable as concrete by any stretch of the imagination, but it would be quick to install and should be easy to care for.

It wasn't the ideal answer to the situation, but it was certainly the most expedient one that would still yield acceptable results.

It might not be everything a girl ever dreamed of, but it was easily a compromise that a grown woman could accept.

CHAPTER 11

"Hey, Suzanne, you aren't closed yet, are you?" Gabby Williams asked me loudly as she stuck her head in the door. In a softer voice, she implored, "Please say yes."

I looked behind Gabby and saw half a dozen kids from two to ten outside, all peering in through my Plexiglas window.

"You're in luck; we're still open. Come on in," I said loudly with a grin.

She shot me an evil look. "Suzanne."

"What? I'm sorry, I couldn't quite hear that last bit you said."

It was too late for her to counter my loud reply. The kids all swarmed into the donut shop and immediately pressed their faces against the display case. Emma and I would have to do double duty on the glass, but it was worth it seeing Gabby so ill at ease. I'd heard that her extended family was in town for New Year's, and these must be from the youngest generation.

They were a mob all by themselves, but Gabby wasn't going to go down without a fight. In a loud voice that would have done a master sergeant proud, she said loudly, "Don't touch the glass. Now line up, from oldest to youngest."

"Aunt Gabby?" one of the smallest of the children asked. "I don't know how many I am."

"You're two, Delaney, so you go to the back of the line," Gabby said.

Anyone who had ever spent time around small children

could have predicted the outcome. It was hard to imagine that loud a wail could come out of such a small package. "It's okay, Delaney. You can have my spot," one of the older girls said.

"Sydney, we'll do things just as I said," Gabby insisted.

The ten-year-old barely looked at her great aunt. "Then she can have my donut." Sydney got down on one knee. "Go ahead, Delaney. Pick one."

"That's not fair," another little girl said from behind the line. "I'm older than *she* is."

"Not by much," a young boy said.

It was complete and utter chaos, and it was all I could do not to smile. Gabby Williams had been known to strike fear into the hearts of residents young and old in April Springs, but she couldn't handle a pack of children without losing complete control.

It was time to step in, not so much to help Gabby as it was to keep these kids from all breaking down into tears.

I walked around from behind the counter and asked, "Who likes donuts?"

"Me!" they all shouted in unison. In Gabby's defense, they were quite loud when they were all talking at the same time.

"The first rule here is that there will be no donuts for anyone who shouts," I said with a wicked grin.

Gabby looked at me as though I'd lost my mind, but I'd dealt with grade school classes full of small kids, so I at least had an idea about what I was doing.

"Now, let's see hands. Donut lovers?"

Every hand shot up, and three kids even put two in the air, but they were all as silent as church mice.

It was nice to see the newfound respect in Gabby's gaze, but if I let her know that I'd seen it, it would vanish quickly enough.

"Very good," I said. It was time to strike quickly now, while I still had them. "We have glazed donuts, chocolate cake donuts, and lemon iced donuts left." I could see them gearing up for arguments about who got what, so I added quickly, "I don't know how you're used to doing it, but at the donut shop, we go by height."

One of the older boys looked smugly at the others. He'd clearly gotten an early growth spurt and was used to holding it over the others, so it was time for my particular twist. "We start with the shortest and work our way up."

There were clouds on the horizon on a few of their faces, but the prospect of protesting and losing their donuts altogether managed to keep them in check, at least for the moment. "Emma, I need some help out here," I called out to my assistant.

She trotted right out, and after she nodded a quick hello to Gabby, she took in all of the children milling around. I warned her not to say a word with a quick glance, so she bit back whatever comment she'd been about to make and asked, "What can I do for you, boss?"

"I'll call the donut out, you bag it, throw in a paper napkin or two, and we'll serve them to go, since we don't have enough seats for this crew. Is that okay with you, Gabby?"

She was stuck, and she knew it. If they ate at my shop, I'd be the one cleaning up the mess, but if she protested that they couldn't get them to go, there would be no donuts, and if that happened, there were going to be some very unhappy children in my shop. I knew Gabby would make me pay for the fun I was having later, but it would be worth every second of it for now. "That will be fine," she said grimly.

"Okay then, we're good to go," I said as I leaned over and spoke to Delaney. "What would you like?"

She smiled at me as though I were Santa and the Easter Bunny all wrapped up in one. "Chocolate."

Emma held up her end, and I handed Delaney her bagged donut. I went to the next little boy in line, and so on and so on, until I got to the very end. "Glazed, please," the young man said with a brief flash of a smile. I had to fight the urge to give him two for being such a good sport, but I knew if I did that, the rabble would be roused again.

After they each had their treats, Gabby approached.

"May I get something for you?" I asked her as sweetly as I could manage.

"No, I believe you've done more than enough today," she replied icily.

"Happy to help. Since you came in so late, the donuts are on the house. In another twenty minutes, I was just going to give them away anyway. Enjoy. You have some great family there, Gabby."

"Thank you," Gabby said, the frost decidedly melting a little in her expression. I knew from experience that she loved a bargain, and it didn't get any better than free.

"You can do it," I told her softly. "Just don't let them see any fear."

"I only wish I could hide it better," she said with a slight smile. Turning back to her grand-nieces and – nephews, Gabby said, "Older ones, take the younger ones by the hand. We're going next door to ReNEWed to enjoy our treats."

"It smells like old people in there," one of the little girls protested.

"Lauren," Gabby said, warning her not to keep saying that.

"Well, it does," the little girl protested.

"May we please just walk next door together without any drama?" she asked them.

I refrained from answering her rhetorical question.

"Come on," an older girl named Katelynn said as she took her little sister's hand. "It will be fun."

It was clear that Gabby didn't think so as she bravely marshaled the troops and left Donut Hearts.

Once Gabby was gone, Emma looked at me and burst out laughing. I couldn't help myself as I joined her in her mirth. I'd been tense ever since I'd found Snappy's body in the donut shop, and it felt good letting a little joy out.

"What was that all about?" Emma asked me once we both caught our breath.

"Evidently Gabby was babysitting an entire generation of her family line, if you can believe that," I said.

"They may not have been able to handle her one on one, but as a group, she was outmatched before she walked in the door."

"I believe you're right," I said as I looked at the nearly empty display cases. "There aren't many donuts left, and I have a full afternoon ahead of me. Why don't we close up a few minutes early and call it a day?"

"It sounds good to me, boss," she said. "There are eighteen donuts left, by my last count. What should we do with them?"

Ordinarily I would have offered them to her, but then I realized we might need some to grease the wheels for our tasks at hand later. "Tell you what, box them in six-packs. I've got a good use for them today."

"Yes, ma'am," Emma said. She did as I asked, and then she took the remaining trays, plates, and other dishes in back to get started on the last round of washing. While she did that, I ran the register reports, and I was pleased when we balanced to the penny.

By the time Jake showed up, three minutes early at that, the shop was closed for the day, Emma had taken the deposit to the bank on her way to school, and everything was put away, ready for Young and his crew to start fixing up Donut Hearts.

"What are those for?" Jake asked as he spied the three half boxes on the counter instantly.

"I thought we might be able to use them as bribes," I explained. "But if you'd like one or two before we go, feel free."

Jake patted his waistline. "No, I believe I'm good. At least I'd better be. I thought your mother and Phillip would be here by now."

I looked outside and saw them approaching. "You know what they say. Speak of the devil and he appears."

"I'm going to tell her that you said that," Jake answered with a laugh.

"Don't worry. I've called her worse over the years, and to her face, too," I replied, grinning as I said it.

"What are you two smiling about?" Momma asked as she and her husband walked into the donut shop.

"It's an inside joke," I said, not wanting to distract any of us from the task at hand. "Do you have the gems with you?"

"Two emeralds apiece, just as promised," she said as she handed me one of the two fancy felt bags in her hand.

"May I?" I asked as I tugged at the drawstring. My curiosity was irresistible.

"Be my guest," my mother said graciously.

I emptied the two stones out onto my hand. They were deep green in appearance, both cut into facets that seemed to magnify their light. Each stone was not much bigger than a pencil eraser, and I had to wonder how much they were worth. "Would it be tacky of me to ask you what these cost?"

"No, of course not. You need to know if you're going to present yourselves as legitimate buyers of more stones. One gem is worth approximately seven thousand dollars, while the other is worth eleven."

"Thousand?" I asked.

"Yes, of course."

Jake studied them a moment. "Funny, but they don't look all that different to me. Why the price difference?"

Momma touched one with her index finger. "This one's a little too dark, and the clarity is a little less as well."

They still looked nearly identical to me, even after her explanation. "You can really see the differences?"

Momma laughed. "I couldn't at first, but I've trained myself to recognize quality stones over the years."

"What do you think of the ones we found here?"

"They were excellent," Momma said.

"Why didn't you mention this expertise yesterday when Suzanne found those jewels?" Jake asked her.

"I wasn't sure it would be appropriate at the time," she said. That was my mother, rarely letting the left hand know what the right was up to.

"And now?"

"We needed emeralds, and I happened to have some in my collection. It's as simple as that. I don't believe there is any way the police chief would have parted with the gems you found, so I offered an alternate solution."

"I'm glad you had them," I said. "They may come in handy."

"One word of caution. Don't let them leave your possession, not for a single moment, no matter how benign the request might seem."

Jake frowned. "Are you afraid of a switch?"

"It's entirely possible," she said.

"Switch?" I asked innocently.

"Some unscrupulous folks have been known to be tempted to appear to examine a good stone, all the while trading it for one of lesser quality," Momma said.

"Wow, it's getting so you can't trust anybody these days," I said with a dry laugh. After all, we were going to be visiting these shops under false pretenses ourselves. The idea that someone might try to take advantage of us at the same time we were doing the same thing to them amused me on a certain level while horrifying me on another. "So, it's settled then. Jake and I will take the two shops in Maple Hollow, and you two will take the three within the area of April Springs. Is everyone still good with that?"

"You know, this might be a fool's errand," Phillip said. "I spoke with Chief Grant, and he drew blanks across the board with his inquiries. Also, there's nothing that says the killer couldn't have taken the stolen gems to Charlotte, or even Atlanta."

"I know, but we can't canvass every pawn store in the south," I replied. "We'll just do the best we can. Who knows? We might get a hit. So far, none of our suspects has ventured out very far, or we would have known about it. We might just get lucky."

"What are those for? Are they extras?" Phillip asked as he spied the donuts as well. What was it about the men in my life that donuts were such a great attractor?

"They're meant to smooth the way. You two can have two boxes, and we'll take the last one."

"And do they each have to have six donuts in them?" the retired chief asked as he lifted one of the lids.

Momma laughed at him. "Try to restrain yourself. We're not going to bribe anyone with a partial box of treats, Phillip. I'm sure if you get peckish, we can pick up some fruit for you along the way."

"Sure. Fruit sounds just as good as donuts," he said with the hint of a frown.

"Why don't we meet back at our place this evening?" Momma suggested. "I've got a big batch of turkey chili simmering away all day in my slow cooker, and I can whip up some fresh biscuits to go with it."

"Sold," Jake said before I could utter a single word. I looked at him for a moment. "What? Suzanne, it would be rude to refuse your mother's invitation."

"Yes, I'm sure that's why you said yes so quickly. It was strictly out of politeness."

"Well, I wouldn't say that was *all* of it," Jake answered as he winked at my mother.

She laughed. "You two are good together, you know that, don't you? Now, if you'll excuse us, Phillip and I have some pawnshops to visit."

"So do we," I said, and we were soon all on our way.

CHAPTER 12

A s Jake drove us to Maple Hollow in his truck, I said, "I'm hesitant to say anything for fear that you'll blow it out of proportion, but something happened this morning at the donut shop you should probably know about." My husband had gotten my Jeep a new battery, so out of gratitude, I'd let him drive again. I hadn't checked the weather report, but how different could it be from what we'd experienced yesterday? Unfortunately, I was about to find out.

"What happened?" he asked as he risked a quick glance in my direction.

"Emma and I were on our break outside when someone drove past the donut shop," I said.

"I realize it's the middle of the night for most folks, but that alone can't be all that unusual. Did you happen to see who was driving?"

"Unfortunately, no. The windows were tinted black, and when I tried to get the license plate after it turned around and went past again, there was a bag over it."

"Could it have just been a coincidence?" Jake asked.

"I didn't think you believed in those," I countered.

"Normally I don't, but whether I like it or not, these things happen sometimes. Did you at least get the make and model?"

"All I can be sure of is that it was a dark sedan. That's all Emma and I could agree on with any certainty, at any rate. So, you don't think it's important?"

"I don't know. We'll keep our eyes open for a dark sedan for now and leave it at that."

"The truth is I feel better just telling you about it," I said.

"Good. That's why I'm here."

"Oh, I can think of a few other reasons," I said with a grin.

"Not while I'm driving, though," he answered with a hint of laughter in his voice.

"Excuse me. We're looking for gemstones," I said as Jake and I walked into the Three Brothers Pawnshop in Maple Hollow. It was in the seedier section of the downtown area, one that had not yet been touched by the urban redevelopers. The shop itself was bright and well lit, with display cases showing everything from handguns to pocket watches to gold lighters neatly displayed, basically an array of everything anyone might want to trade in for cash, either for a short-term loan or as an outright sale. Guitars lined the section of the wall behind the man I'd learned was the manager, and I wondered if there were any left in town, since there was such a vast supply of them there.

"We've got our diamonds, rubies, and emeralds over here," he said as he showed us a selection of rings, pendants, and earrings. "What's your pleasure?"

"Sorry, I should have been more specific," I said. "We're interested in loose emeralds. Have you had any come in over the last day or two?"

The owner's gaze narrowed for an instant, and I saw his smile grow to a thin line. "Not lately, no."

"Do you have any in stock at all?" Jake asked him.

"You're a cop, aren't you? Don't you guys ever talk to each other? Your buddies were already here."

"I'm not a police officer," Jake said emphatically.

The man continued to size him up, and it was clear he didn't believe him. "Maybe not, but you used to be, and not that long ago, either, unless I'm wrong, and the thing is, I'm never wrong about stuff like that."

How was it that folks who lived on the shadier side of the street were so good about picking up on the fact that Jake used to be a law enforcement officer? Was it the way he spoke, the way he carried himself, or something even more subtle than that? Whatever the reason, it had happened more than once when we'd been together, and I knew if Jake continued to be a part of my investigations, it would continue to occur.

"Okay, you got me, but I'm retired. I'm just a plain old civilian now."

The man didn't seem as though he believed him, so I handed him the donuts I'd brought with me to ease our way. "I myself am a donut maker, and if you want any more proof than that, here you go."

"I'm not looking to buy any donuts, lady."

"That's good, because these are on the house," I said.

"Seriously?" he asked as he looked steadily at me, as though it were something I'd lie about.

"Seriously," I said with a grin. "Help yourself."

Judging from the man's massive girth, he had never said no to a confectionary treat in his life. He flipped open the lid and immediately wolfed down the closest donut to him. I wasn't even sure he'd been able to taste it, but he smiled at me with real satisfaction as he licked the icing off his fingers. "That was first rate."

"Thanks," I said. "Now, about those emeralds."

He looked around at the nearly empty shop, and then he lowered his voice as he explained, "Like I told the cop who came in earlier, nobody's brought any stones by."

"Okay," I said.

Before I could ask a follow-up question, he added, "Somebody did call an hour ago, though. They had half a dozen emeralds they wanted to sell, and quick."

"Did you happen to catch a name? Was it a man or a woman?" Jake asked in rapid order.

"I didn't take the call; one of my people did. My nephew isn't the brightest bulb, if you know what I mean. I asked him about it, but he couldn't even say whether it was a man or a woman. Evidently the person on the other end was whispering, and sometimes it's hard to make anything out."

"Is the seller coming by later, by any chance?" I asked.

"My guess is no. Evidently they'd never done business with a pawnshop before, at least one that was on the up and up. Billy told the caller that they'd have to provide a photo ID before we could buy anything from them, and as soon as he said that, they hung up on him. We get those calls every now and then. Amateur thieves most likely, and we don't go out of our way looking for trouble with the police or anyone else. We do our best to run a clean business here. Sorry I couldn't help more."

"You've done plenty, well worth the price of half a dozen donuts," I told him with a smile. I gave him a business card for the donut shop and jotted my cell phone number on the back of it. "If they happen to change their minds and come in, give me a call. There's another dozen donuts in it for you if you do."

"With a payoff like that, I'll make sure my entire staff knows."

Once we were outside, I asked Jake, "What do you make of that?"

"It's pretty clear at this point that we're dealing with an amateur, and they can be unpredictable. But we already knew that, didn't we? I'm curious to see what the next place has to say." Jake smiled for a moment before he added, "Those donuts were magic, weren't they?"

"They can be," I said. "Are you sorry I gave Momma the last two boxes?"

"It couldn't be helped, but now we're going to have to rely on our charm instead of your treats."

"Wow, then we could be in trouble," I answered with a laugh.

The other pawnshop in town was quite a bit shadier than the one we'd just visited. It was tough getting into the place for all of the lawnmowers and chainsaws stacked out front, and once we were inside, I had a difficult time seeing anything. Whereas the last place had been brightly lit, this one was dark and creepy. There had been some order and organization at the first pawnshop as well. Here, things had clearly been placed in random order with no thought given to anything but expediency.

"Let me handle this," Jake said.

"Sure," I replied, wondering what he had in mind.

"We need to see your latest unmounted emerald purchases," Jake demanded when we found the woman in charge.

"You guys need to stop pestering me. You're bad for business. This place has been crawling with cops today. People are going to start talking."

Jake took the bag of Momma's stones out of his pocket and emptied them into his hand. "We're not fooling around here," he said, and it took me a moment to realize that Jake hadn't corrected the woman's assumption that he was an officer of the law.

"Let me see those," the pawnshop dealer said as she reached for them.

Jake was too quick for her, though. "I don't think so. Now answer my question. Have you taken any in?"

"Nope," she said with a grumble as she continued to stare at the stones in Jake's possession.

I hoped he'd put them away, and he finally did so, much to the woman's chagrin.

"Have you had any telephone calls about emeralds, by any chance?" I asked her.

She looked at me for a moment, and then she dismissed me as being unimportant once she realized that I wasn't a cop. "Nobody's called about loose precious stones in months. Look around. It's not exactly our usual trade. Now if you were looking for an old chainsaw or a weed eater that barely works, I'd be your gal. But emeralds? Hardly."

"You wouldn't lie to us, now would you?" Jake asked her in a deadly soft voice.

"No way. There's no money in it for me. Now if we're done here, I've got work to do."

Once we were outside, Jake said, "If it's any consolation, I don't think six dozen donuts would have done us any good in there."

"Do you believe her?" I asked him.

"I'm not even sure *she* knows when she's lying or telling the truth these days," he replied. "The truth of the matter is that it was the reaction I'd been expecting all along. She protested a little too much about her inventory, if you ask me. In the past, it's been my experience that pawnshop dealers are notorious for skirting the law, and they aren't all that fond of cops in general."

"How do they all seem to know you were a cop once?" I asked him. I'd speculated on it earlier, but I suddenly realized that I'd never come right out and asked him about it.

"I suppose you get a way of looking at suspicious people a certain way," Jake explained, "and it happens nearly as soon as you graduate from the academy. Sure, it could be the way I handle myself, but they *know* I'm sizing them up, and there's nothing I can do to disguise it. Half the time I'm not even aware that I'm doing it. It couldn't be any clearer if we were all wearing name tags, though."

"Interesting. Hey, I'm getting hungry. How about you?"

"I could eat," he admitted. "Should we go back to Burt's, or do you want to head back to April Springs now that our pawnshop visits are over?"

"I'd like to stay in town a little longer, if it's all the same to you," I admitted. "I spoke with two of our suspects today, but I'd like a crack at the other two, since we're already here."

"Burt's it is, then," Jake said.

As we drove to the diner, I asked my husband, "Do you think those emeralds are ever going to show up, or is the killer going to just hold onto them now that they know selling them won't be as easy as they must have first suspected?"

"No, they'll be sold before too long, unless I miss my guess," Jake said.

"Why do you say that?"

"Think about it, Suzanne. It's the only way it makes sense, at least as far as I'm concerned. I can't imagine the killer is going to want to keep evidence around that they killed Snappy any longer than they have to, and besides, my gut is telling me that the emeralds were the motive for the murder itself. Somebody needs money, and badly. That's where we should be looking."

"How did you manage to come up with that?"

"I wasn't a cop for so many years without picking up a thing or two along the way," he said with a wry laugh.

"I wasn't questioning your ability," I said quickly. "I'm just surprised by how your mind works sometimes."

"I've tasted some of your creations at the donut shop," Jake said. "Was there always a logical reason behind some of the combinations you've created over the years?"

"No, some of it was just instinct," I admitted.

"Or, put another way, you internally extrapolated based on

past experience until you subconsciously came up with a flavor combination that met the requirements of providing a possible new and improved taste palette for your customer base."

"Wow, when you put it that way, I sound like a culinary genius," I said with a grin.

"In a way, it's what we both do. We feed our subconscious with seemingly unrelated facts until we can form conclusions based on previous observations. It sounds scientific because it is, at least as far as I'm concerned."

I frowned a little. "It takes a little of the fun out of spontaneous creation when you look at it that way," I said.

"Not at all. There are always jumps of reasoning and flashes of insight that overrule all of that. What you do is art, but there can also be underlying rationales for the things you create."

"You seem to have given this a lot of thought," I said.

"Hey, I'm off the clock these days, remember? Time is one thing I've got plenty of."

I was about to suggest we figure something out he could do next with his life when our conversation was cut short by our arrival at the diner.

It would be a discussion for another day, but sooner rather than later.

Right now we had a murder to solve, and things weren't getting any easier with each passing moment.

CHAPTER 13

"**H**EY, TAMMY. IS SOMETHING WRONG?" I asked the waitress at Burt's after she came over to our table to take our order. Her usual lively personality was subdued, and she barely made eye contact when I spoke.

"I'm fine," she said brusquely. "What can I get for you today?"

"Two specials, assuming they're different from our last meal," Jake said, trying to ease her out of her mood.

She didn't take the bait as she jotted our order down and started for the kitchen.

"Was it something I said?" Jake asked as he looked at me.

I kept watching her, and then I pointed to a man sitting alone in a booth in one corner. He wasn't eating the food in front of him; he was simply staring holes through our waitress. Tammy had picked up a few dirty plates on her way back to the kitchen, and when she glanced his way, she nearly dropped them. "Something's going on there," I said softly.

"It's none of our business, Suzanne," Jake said evenly. "We already have enough troubles without getting involved in her life, too."

"Something's not right; that's all I'm saying," I said.

Tammy came back with our sweet teas, which we hadn't ordered, and set them down in front of us.

"Is he bothering you?" I asked her gently.

"I don't know what you're talking about," she said. "Now, if you'll excuse me, I'm going on break. Kathy will take care of you." Tammy practically sprinted toward the kitchen, and I half expected the strange man to get up and follow her, but he just sat there.

I lost track of him after our food came, and at one point I looked up from my country-style fried steak and saw that he was gone. "Did you happen to notice that man leave?"

"Who are you talking about? That guy from before?" Jake asked as he bit into another morsel. The meat was done to perfection, and I had a hunch we'd found the cook's specialty, purely by accident. The entrée was crisp on the outside and yet still tender and juicy inside. I found it delicious, but I still couldn't get Tammy's reaction out of my mind.

"Never mind," I said. After we finished eating and we paid our bill, Jake started for the truck. I looked up at the gray clouds above us and realized that it was beginning to snow, something that surprised me.

"Did you know we were supposed to get snow today?" I asked him.

He held out a hand and watched a few flakes fall into it. "No, but I don't mind it. It's a lot better than ice."

"Sure, but Young's work crew is supposed to be fixing the outside of the donut shop tomorrow," I said.

"Don't worry about it. It probably won't amount to much."

My husband kept walking toward the truck when a nagging sense of dread came over me. "Hang on a second, Jake."

As I started off in the other direction, heading for the alley behind the diner, he said, "We're parked out front; you know that, right?"

"Indulge me," I said. I walked down the alley, and soon I heard voices coming from the back of the diner before we even saw who exactly was in the middle of an argument.

"Keep your mouth shut," the man was yelling at Tammy,

and worse yet, he had a hand clamped down on her arm that was clearly hurting her.

I didn't have to say a word to Jake. He took off like a shot, and before I knew what was happening, my husband had broken the man's grip on Tammy's arm, and he had him pinned up against the back of the diner.

Tammy started crying, and I moved in to comfort her as I heard my husband tell the man, "You need to walk away, and I mean right now. If you bother her again, you'll have to answer to me. Do you understand everything I'm telling you, and is there any doubt in your mind that I'm telling you the truth?"

"You think you're so tough," the stranger said, spitting out his words. He was clearly humiliated by the ease with which Jake had handled him, and he was trying to cover up his fear as well.

"As a matter of fact, I do. I don't have to go around grabbing women to prove I'm a real man, so I suppose that makes me tougher than you."

"Don't kid yourself. You got lucky. You caught me off guard," the man protested as he brushed some of the falling snow out of his hair.

Jake grinned at him, but there wasn't an ounce of joy in it. He released the man and took two steps backward, never wavering from staring him down. "You're welcome to try me again if you honestly feel that way. Are you ready to take a run at me now, or do you need a little more time to work up your nerve?"

"Lester, just go home," Tammy pled with the man.

"I'll go when I'm good and ready," Lester said.

"Yeah, Lester and I aren't finished with our conversation," Jake said. Was my husband actually egging the man into trying something? I knew he hated bullies with a passion, and Lester was clearly one with every ounce of his being. However, I knew that the thing with most bullies, not all but most, was that when they were pushed, they usually backed down. Only those who wouldn't fight back became their victims. "What do you say, Lester? Want to continue our little chat?"

"Forget you," Lester said as he brushed past Jake, trying to knock him off balance with his shoulder.

Jake must have seen it coming from a mile away. He stood his ground firmly, and it was Lester who lost his balance and nearly fell onto the suddenly slippery pavement when he collided with my husband. He would have done a face plant into the asphalt, too, if Jake hadn't reached out and grabbed him nearly at the same spot where Lester had manhandled Tammy a moment ago. "Careful there, Lester, you'd hate to fall and hurt yourself."

I expected Jake to give the man's arm an extra little squeeze before he released it, but he touched him as delicately as he would have handled a rose. Lester looked surprised by the action as well.

He was gone in a moment, and then and only then did Jake turn to the waitress. "Are you okay, Tammy?"

"I'm fine," she said, rubbing her arm self-consciously.

"Was that your boyfriend?" I asked her lightly.

"No, that's my big brother," she said, shocking me with her response. "He wanted money so he could get drunk, but I refused, and he got nasty."

"I could always have the chief of police here in town speak with him," Jake said. "Or, if you'd prefer, if he bothers you again, you can call me and I'll be here in under twenty minutes to take care of the situation."

"Thanks for the offer, but he's not hanging around. Lester is going to visit a friend in California, and he spent the last of his money on a bus ticket. That's why he wanted some cash for booze. In an hour, he'll be someone else's problem."

"I'm so sorry you had to go through that," I said. "I never had a brother, or a sister, either, for that matter."

"Then count yourself lucky," Tammy said. She clearly felt

uncomfortable with us seeing her in such a vulnerable position, because she quickly added, "I need to get back inside. My break's over."

"I meant what I said. Call me if you need me," Jake told her.

"What are you, my knight in shining armor?" Tammy asked him, breaking out a bit of her old smile for just a moment.

"Actually, he's mine, but I'll let you borrow him any time if you need to," I told her.

"I appreciate that," she said. Tammy headed for the back door, but before she went inside, she added, "As my way of saying thanks, your next slice of pie is on the house."

"You shouldn't have told him that," I said to her. "Now he'll want to eat here again tonight."

Tammy laughed, and then the waitress started to go back inside. "You wanted to know about Snappy yesterday, didn't you?"

"That's why we're here," I said.

"I don't know anything yet, but I'll keep my eyes and ears open."

"We'd appreciate that," I said, and then she vanished back into Burt's.

After she was gone, I kissed Jake's cheek and said, "Thank you."

"For what?"

"For what? How about sticking up for someone who was in trouble? Isn't that enough?"

"He wasn't a threat to me, Suzanne. Lester's just like a thousand other punks I've seen in my life trying to scare people with how tough he pretends to be."

"I doubt he'll try that again anytime soon."

"I wouldn't count on that if I were you," Jake said.

He seemed sad by the need to show force now that it was over. "At least he won't pick on Tammy again," I said lamely.

"Not from California, so at least there's that," Jake said as we started walking back to the front of Burt's so we could get into his truck and go. The snow was beginning to pick up, and I hoped that it hadn't been a mistake letting him drive. He could haul a lot more than I could, but my vehicle could climb a tree, whereas his truck sometimes got stuck in a heavy dew.

"What now?" Jake asked. "Should we go see what our other two suspects are up to? I'd like to find out about their finances while we're at it."

"If greed is the true motive for Snappy's murder, maybe we'll find something, but let's hold off before we track them down."

"What did you have in mind?"

"I'm not without my sources in town, remember?" I asked. "Let's ask if Adam Jefferson or Meredith Pence have any idea about what's really going on with their money situations. We know Deloris is close to broke, and it shouldn't be too hard to ask those two about Sanderson, Bloch, and Madison, and their money situations." I looked up into the sky and saw the snow was really starting to intensify. "Do you think we'll be okay hanging around with this stuff falling so fast and so thick?"

Jake smiled. "No worries on that count. I've got enough weight in back to keep our rear end on the road. We'll be fine."

"If you say so," I said, wondering if we'd make it back to April Springs, or if we'd have to call someone to come get us.

"Adam, do you have a minute?" I asked when we returned to the attorney's office. For once, he made an impressive figure in his three-piece suit, as opposed to his usual handyman garb.

"Just about that," he said after he greeted us in return. "I'm due in court in ten minutes, so if you want to walk over there with me, we can chat on the way."

"It's about Snappy Mack," I said, but before I could get into any details, he interrupted me.

"Guys, I wish I could help you, I really do, but my hands are tied. I was a great friend of your aunt's, Suzanne, but I wouldn't break a client's confidence, even for her."

"How about this?" Jake suggested as Adam locked his office and started off on foot toward the courthouse. "We'll ask you questions, and if you can't answer for whatever reason, we'll drop that line of our questioning."

"That sounds reasonable enough," Adam agreed.

"Do you know anything about the finances of Sanderson Mack?" I asked. "Is he in good shape financially, or is he barely getting by?"

"It's no secret that his business failed late last year," the attorney told us. "I've heard rumors that his loans are coming due soon, but I can't say for sure one way or the other."

"Okay, that's good," I said, happy that at least Snappy's son wasn't the attorney's client, or he wouldn't have been able to comment at all.

"I don't see who it serves that the man is facing some serious financial ramifications for his questionable business practices, but if it makes you happy, fine then."

"That's not what she meant," Jake said, rushing to my defense.

"Take it easy," Adam said with a smile. "I know what she meant. I suppose it's true. Sanderson had a motive for killing his father, but only if he inherits his assets, which is yet to be determined at this point."

"Still, he could have seen it as his only way out if he believed he was getting everything," I prodded.

"It's possible," the attorney conceded.

"Moving on, what do you know about Madison Moore?" I asked.

"She's trouble, plain and simple. The young lady has always had champagne taste on a beer budget. I know from firsthand experience that she's overextended on her credit cards, and not just a little, either. I happened to be in court last month waiting for a case to be called when a local business sued her for nonpayment. Evidently her credit history is a long and complicated series of extensions and cash advances that would curl any normal person's toes."

"How about Snappy's business he owned with Hank Bloch?" Jake asked.

"I have no idea what their finances were like as a company," the attorney said. "Only that Snappy had assets on his own."

So we'd covered all of the suspects except Deloris Mack. "And Snappy's ex-wife?" I asked him, just to confirm our earlier suspicion that he was representing one of our suspects.

Instead of answering the question directly, the attorney glanced at his watch. "I'm sorry I can't give you more time, but I need to get into the zone for this case. Happy hunting."

With that, Adam hurried his pace in order to get away from us as quickly as possible.

Jake started after him when I touched my husband's shoulder. "Let him go."

"Don't you think we can push him a little harder?" Jake asked. "I have a feeling he knows more than he's letting on."

"Why should he be any different than anyone else?" I asked him. "Frankly, I was amazed by how forthcoming he was with us."

"I don't know," Jake said doubtfully.

"That's because you're used to being able to compel someone to talk to you. Everything on this side is done purely on a volunteer basis."

"I get it. So, we now know that three of our four suspects had financial motive to want to see Snappy dead, and any one of them could have been at the donut shop to ask him for money when they discovered him with the emeralds. I'd still like to know more about Hank Bloch and what his individual status is like."

"So would I," I said. "That's why we're going to the library."

"What do you think Meredith can tell us today that she didn't mention yesterday?" Jake asked me as we headed for his truck, the snow continuing to fall all around us.

"I'm not sure, but if anyone knows what's going on in this town, I'm willing to bet she's the one. She's like any other good librarian; she might not know herself, but I'm willing to bet that she'll know who to ask."

CHAPTER 14

"MEREDITH, WE HATE TO BOTHER you again, but could you spare us a few minutes of your time?" I asked her.

"Of course, but I'm sorry to say that I have nothing new to add to our conversation from yesterday," she said apologetically. "I'd love to be able to help you find out who killed my uncle, but I'm out of information on the topic."

"Actually, we're interested in learning how his construction company is doing," I said. "Would you have any idea?"

"Do you mean financially? That's a little out of my purview," she said.

"I knew it might be, but who better to ask than a librarian?" I asked her with a smile.

"Flattery is nice, but I still can't answer the question." Meredith paused for a moment, looked around the large expanse, and then she said, "Follow me."

Jake looked at me with his eyebrows raised, but all I could do was shrug. Evidently Meredith had an idea, but she clearly didn't feel any desire to explain what it was. The three of us walked through the main library together, down some stairs into the basement, and into a glass-enclosed room that had the word Genealogy emblazoned across the door. At first, it appeared that the room was empty, but then I saw a white-haired older man stand up from behind one of the desks. He might have been late in years, but he had an instant air about him that shouted his vitality. There was no stoop to his shoulders, and his eyes were both bright and clear.

"Carter, do you have a second?" Meredith asked him.

"What do any of us have but the continuous ticking of the clock toward our individual fates?" the man said rather poetically. Did he always talk like that? If he did, he must be tedious to have a conversation with.

"Indeed," Meredith said with a smile. It was clear from the start that she was fond of the man and vice versa. "I thought you might be able to help my friends out."

"Sorry, but we don't need information on anyone's family tree," I said apologetically.

"Everyone should know where they come from," he said to me with an indulgent smile. "How else can they possibly know where they are going?"

"Suzanne, Jake, I'd like you to meet Carter Wills. Carter, this is Jake and Suzanne Hart."

"Actually, he's Jake Bishop. I'm still going by Hart for the donut shop's sake."

"Would that be Donut Hearts, by any chance?" Carter asked, his eyes lighting up.

"Guilty as charged," I said with a grin.

"I've sampled your delightful treats. They are amazing!"

"Thanks so much. It's always nice to meet a fan," I told him.

"Can we get back to our question?" Jake asked, interrupting the warm and fuzzy turn our conversation had taken. "We're inquiring about the financial state of the construction company recently run by Snappy Mack and Hank Bloch."

"I'll leave you to it," Meredith said as she excused herself.

"Thanks," I told her. "We'll check in on the way out."

"Good, I'd like that."

After the librarian was gone, Jake asked Carter, "Would you

mind telling us why Meredith would believe you might be able to help us?"

"It's simple enough. Before I retired last month and began to devote myself to my lifelong interest of genealogy, I worked at the building inspection office for the county."

"And how does that relate to the construction company's status?" I asked.

He laughed. "You clearly have no ties to the building trade. It is made up of a group of the worst gossips I've ever had the pleasure of knowing in my life. Nothing, and I mean nothing, escaped my attention while I was there."

"So, do you know anything about Hank Bloch?" Jake asked him.

"The man loves to gamble, and I don't mean just on deadlines and low bids. From what I've heard, he is in debt up to his eyebrows to several of the less savory elements of the trade, and from what I've heard, their patience is wearing thin with him as they wait for repayment."

I looked at Jake, who nodded at me. "That's excellent news, though not for Hank," my husband said. "When we spoke with him yesterday, he was under the impression that he's set to inherit everything Snappy owned, including some personal property that was worth quite a bit."

"I believe he's simply foolishly grasping at straws," Carter said with a frown.

"Why is that?"

"It is common knowledge that Snappy used his wealth as a whip on the people around him. From what I understand, he tended to change his will at the drop of a hat. Who knows which version was the latest? I told him on more than one occasion that it was foolish to give anyone a reason to believe that he was worth more to them dead than he ever would be alive, but he wouldn't listen to me. It was a game to him, as dangerous as it turned out to be. All I could do was offer him my warning. Ultimately, our behavior is up to each of us and no one else."

"Do you happen to know anything about Deloris, Snappy's ex-wife?" Jake asked him out of the blue. Evidently we weren't finished with the retiree quite yet.

"Quite a bit, actually." Was the man actually blushing? "I don't suppose there was any reason for Meredith to mention it, but we've been seeing each other for several months."

That was news. "You and Deloris?" I asked. I hadn't meant to make it sound so outlandish a proposition, but it must have sounded that way to Carter.

He wasn't upset, merely bemused by my question. "I know, we make an unlikely pair, but we've each been unlucky in love in the past, and yet somehow we found our way to each other among a sea of strangers."

"I know the question is impertinent, and feel free not to answer, but by any chance were the two of you together the night before last?" Jake asked him bluntly.

"You're looking for an alibi, aren't you? For her or for me?" Carter asked. "You see, I realize to an outsider, I may have just admitted to a motive of my own for the benefit of Snappy Mack's ex."

"He didn't mean it that way," I said, but Jake just shrugged.

Carter chose to laugh instead of being insulted by the implication. "Shake my hand, sir."

Jake, surprised, did as he was told, and Carter took it gladly. "Why that particular reaction to my question?"

"The county was clearly finished with me, and the implication when I was forced into retirement was that I should go find a corner somewhere and wait to die. You've just given me a vibrant, if completely imaginary, compelling argument to commit murder, and for love, no less. It's more excitement than I usually get, even if it is all pure fabrication and speculation."

"Can you prove it, though?"

Carter frowned for a moment, and then he laughed. "I'm betting that us being together all night won't be enough for you. What timeframe are we discussing here?"

"Sometime between eleven p.m. and three a.m.," Jake said. The chief had been able to narrow it down to those hours, we'd just recently learned.

"We're both covered, then. Deloris and I were visiting my daughter in Tennessee, a fact she will gladly swear to in court. Hannah is not a big fan of my lady friend, so she'd have no reason to lie to protect her, even for me." Carter grabbed a piece of paper and jotted down a telephone number. "Call her."

"We'll do that," Jake said.

Clearly, it wasn't good enough for the amateur genealogist. "I mean right now, before I've had a chance to warn my daughter regarding what you might ask her." There was a gleam in his eyes as he said it, a gauntlet thrown at our feet.

Doing as was suggested, Jake pulled out his phone and made the call. After a brief conversation, he hung up and turned to me. "It holds, unless his daughter is in on it, too."

"My, you're suspicious of everyone, aren't you?" Carter asked with delight.

"Sometimes that's what it takes," Jake said.

"Well, if there's anything else I can do for you, don't hesitate to ask," he said as he turned back to an open book on the table in front of him.

"Since you offered, can you give us any insight into Sanderson Mack or Madison Moore?" I asked him.

"Sanderson is weak, both morally and physically. For him to drive a screwdriver through his father's back and skewer his heart is almost beyond comprehension."

"Unless he was enraged by something," Jake added softly.

"There's always that," Carter said, agreeing with a nod.

"And Madison?" I asked.

"I would put nothing, and I mean nothing, past that young lady. She is a prettily wrapped present with nothing but rotten vileness inside."

"You sound as though you're speaking from experience with her," I said gently.

"Indirectly. She broke my only son's bank account, and then she managed to do the same to his spirit. She drained him for all he was worth, and then she discarded him like some empty container. If Madison had been murdered, I would have surely been on your list of suspects, though no doubt it would have been a long and colorful collection by the time you finished compiling it."

Jake was ready to go, but I wasn't, not until I asked him an important question, at least to me. "How's your son doing now?"

"How kind of you to ask," Carter said with a gentle smile. "Paul has recovered, both his credit and his mental health. He married a lovely young woman named Tina, and they are quite happy together these days. Thank you for asking."

"Thank you for all of the time you've given us," I said.

Carter was about to respond when the door to the genealogy room opened, and Meredith came in, looking rather grim. "I'm sorry to interrupt, but we're closing the library. The storm is getting worse, so if you two want to get back to April Springs, I suggest you go now."

Out on the sidewalk, Jake looked up at the disquieting sky. "What do you think?"

"I think we're going to be in trouble if we hang around Maple Hollow too long," I said. "Should we head back now?"

"The roads aren't that bad yet," Jake said as he scuffed his shoe across the pavement. "Why don't we go find Madison and

Sanderson and see what they have to say before we panic and hit the road before we have to?"

"Okay, if you're sure," I said, though the sky wasn't getting any brighter, and I had a hunch that the weather was just going to get worse as the afternoon progressed.

We drove to Sanderson's place, but there was no response to our summons.

"Could he possibly be at work?" I asked Jake.

"His business went under, remember? Maybe he's just ducking us."

Jake skipped the doorbell this time and pounded on the door with his closed fist, hammering away at it far longer than I would have.

There was still no answer.

"This is hopeless," I said. "Let's go find Madison's place and then get out of town while we still can."

Jake agreed. "Who knows? Maybe they're together again."

"Do you honestly think they're seeing each other so soon after Snappy died?"

"She appears to be the type to move on to the next person in line, and if it's Sanderson, I don't think she's going to have a bit of a problem managing it."

"That presupposes she knows that she's not getting any of the money herself, though," I replied as we headed to her address. I'd looked it up during a lull at the donut shop earlier, so I knew where she currently lived.

Whether she was there or not was a completely different matter.

"Maybe she's hedging *all* of her bets," Jake said.

"You don't think much of her, do you?"

"I've seen users like her before, Suzanne," he said quietly.

"From firsthand experience?"

"No, thankfully, that was one trap I never managed to fall into. Some of my worst cases as an investigator were spurred on by artificial jealousy stoked by someone who was after something. The combination of love and greed can be pretty powerful."

As we drove, I looked over at the profound sadness in my husband, and it hurt my heart to see it. "Sometimes I forget what you had to endure before."

He patted my knee affectionately. "It's fine. After all, it made me always appreciate what I've got," Jake said with a smile.

"Me, too, though I can't compare war stories with you."

"I don't know. I imagine things can get pretty rough when you're running low on donuts at the shop," he said with a laugh.

"Not as much as you might think. If my stock starts to run dry, I just lock the door and hide in the kitchen until everyone goes away."

"That's what I'd do, given the choice," Jake said as he started to park the truck at the apartment complex in question where Madison resided. He skidded a little on the snowy pavement, and for a moment, I wasn't sure he'd be able to stop, but Jake quickly got it under control and managed to halt our progress before we wound up in someone's living room.

"Whew, that was a close call," I said.

"That? Nonsense. I never lost control for one second."

I looked at him skeptically. "So, you're trying to tell me that you *meant* to slide into the spot?"

"What can I say? Sometimes I'm a bit of a showman."

"Come on, let's go see if she's home," I answered.

"What are you two doing here?" Madison Moore asked as she answered the door. She'd obviously been napping, and her hair was mussed, her makeup in need of touching up.

"We came to see you," I said brightly, happy for some reason that I'd caught her at less than her best. "May we come in?"

"This isn't a good time," she said, glancing back inside her place. Was it possible that Sanderson was inside, cowering in a closet?

"It won't take long. We were wondering if you've been able to come up with any reason someone would want to see your boyfriend dead that you couldn't come up with before. After all, you've had some time to think about it and get over the initial shock of it all."

"I don't think I'll ever get over that," she said. "But no, Snappy was such a sweetheart, I can't imagine anyone wanting to kill him."

"He was certainly good to you, wasn't he?" I asked.

"What do you mean by that?"

"You told us that he gave you that brand-new car, and not a cheap one by the look of it. Don't forget, he also said that he was going to leave you a fortune; isn't that what you told us yesterday? That should really be able to help with that crushing credit card debt you're facing."

I got a direct flash of hot contempt from her for a moment before she was able to subdue it and rein it back in. "It's a common enough problem these days. What can I say? The economy got me, just as it did just about everyone else."

"Madison?" I heard a man's voice call out from the other room. "Who is it?"

"I'll be right there," she said before turning back to us. "I'm having a meeting with my accountant, so if you'll excuse me..."

We didn't get a chance to answer, as the door was slammed in our faces.

"For some reason, I don't think that was really her accountant," Jake said with a grin. "I suspect it might have been Sanderson himself, but I'm not entirely sure of it."

"What should we do?"

"Normally, I'd say we stake the place out until whoever is

in there leaves, but I have to admit, I'm not crazy about this weather myself."

"At least we're in agreement on that," I said. "This can wait another day."

As we got back into the truck, instead of leaving the apartment complex, Jake started driving slowly around the parking area. "What are you looking for?"

"I'm wondering if Bloch's work truck might be tucked away somewhere discreetly," Jake admitted. "It wouldn't surprise me one bit if Madison was playing more than one angle right now."

We'd gone halfway through the complex when I put a hand on his arm. "Stop!"

"What is it? Did you see the truck?"

I pointed to a car that looked very familiar to me. "That looks exactly like the car that did a drive-by past the donut shop this morning."

"How can you be sure? I didn't think you got that good a look at it," Jake asked.

He was right, of course. It looked similar, but then I realized that a few others parked nearby could have just as easily been the vehicle in question too, or none of them at all, for that matter. "I didn't, and I can't," I said, feeling suddenly deflated. "I suppose I'm just jumping at shadows now."

"It's okay," Jake said, backing up the truck until we were behind the car in question. "The bag's gone, if it's the same one. That figures."

"They couldn't very well drive here from April Springs with it still over the license plate," I said. "I'm probably wrong. Jake, we really do need to head back home."

He looked up at the sky again through the windshield, and then he quickly nodded. "You're right. I don't want to risk it any longer." His wife and his unborn child had died in a car wreck years before, though snow hadn't played a role in the accident, so I wasn't surprised when he'd finally agreed to go. In fact, I'd been a little shocked when he hadn't insisted that we leave town at the sign of the first snowflake coming down.

The road got continuously worse as we headed out of town instead of any better. Jake's windshield wipers were beating in quick time trying to keep up with the falling snow, but they were failing miserably at their assigned task. At least there weren't many people out on the road with us. It appeared that most folks had had the good sense to stay home. As we rounded a bend in the road, I could feel the truck begin to slide off the shoulder. One glance through my window showed a steep drop-off on the passenger side at least fifteen feet below the road itself, and I wondered, if we continued to slide, if anyone would find us down there. It was a chilling thought, lying at the bottom of the gulley, trapped and unable to get out.

"Jake?"

No answer from him.

I glanced over at him and saw that his knuckles were white on the wheel as he steered into the skid, trying to correct our slide. I knew intellectually that it was the right thing to do, but emotionally, it felt as though he was sending us straight over the side.

His correction didn't work, though, and I felt us getting closer and closer to the brink of oblivion.

CHAPTER 15

I F IT HAD BEEN JUST pavement all the way to the edge of the precipice, there was no doubt in my mind that we would have gone over, but the berm had been graveled and banked a bit, offering us a slight incline before we ventured over the edge. It didn't look like much, but it was just enough to stop us from sliding a little on the built-up gravel, and the truck finally righted itself under Jake's expert hand, just in time.

"That was closer than I'd ever care to admit," Jake said once he was going in the right direction again. He glanced over at me, but for just a moment. "Were you scared?"

"Not in the least," I said, lying as much as I ever had in my life.

Jake shook his head once, and then he burst out laughing. I had no choice; I joined him. Once we had that release of frivolity, we both felt better.

And then the oddest thing happened.

The snow ended.

I don't mean that it slowly tapered off, getting less and less with each passing yard.

I mean it ended.

It was as though a line had been drawn on the surface of the world around us. One side had an inch of snow on it, and the other had barely been touched by any of it. "Wow, I've seen a demarcation like that with rain, but never with snow," Jake said.

"It's pretty cool, isn't it?" I asked as we were suddenly in the clear. "That was some fancy driving you did back there."

"I've never been happier in my life that they made me take that defensive driving course in the academy," he replied with a grin. "I'm glad we got out of town when we did."

"So am I," I said. The sky went from somber gray clouds to a clear blue expanse, dotted occasionally with wisps of white clouds, and I actually felt the sun on the side of my face through the windshield. "It appears that April Springs is going to dodge that particular bullet."

"It's a good thing, too," Jake said as his grip on the steering wheel eased up considerably now that we were in the clear. "They're working on your exterior tomorrow, aren't they?"

"That's what Young said, but I can't imagine that he'll be able to do much with the interior in one day."

"Do you want to stop by before we go by your mother's place and see how it's going?" Jake asked me with a grin.

I was tempted, but I knew better than to push the contractor with my presence. "Let's wait until later. Maybe he'll be gone by the time we finish eating."

"That sounds reasonable enough," Jake said. "I wonder if Dorothea and Phillip had any more luck than we did this afternoon. We might just as well have stayed home, for all the good our investigation did us."

"How can you say that? We found out that Deloris has an alibi, Sanderson, Madison, and Bloch all have motives for the immediate need for money, and we suspect that Madison is canoodling with at least one other man, and quite possibly more, less than forty-eight hours after her boyfriend was murdered. I don't know how they look at progress with the state police, but I'd say we had a remarkable day."

Jake grinned at me. "You're right. I probably just expect too much from myself."

"Well, knock it off, would you?" I asked with a grin. "We're doing great."

"Okay, I agree," he answered. "We're a regular whirlwind. I just wish things would move a little faster, that's all."

"You're thinking like a professional now instead of an unpaid investigator," I reminded him. "We have so few of the tools you used to, I'm amazed by how well we manage to do. If I were a betting woman, I'd say that Momma and Phillip found at least one pawnbroker who got a call about emeralds over the last couple of days, too. How about you? Care to make a wager?"

"No bet. I think you're right. Whoever's sitting on those emeralds must be getting awfully antsy about now." Jake took the packet of two emeralds Momma had loaned us and handed them to me. "I don't even like carrying *these* around, and we got them legitimately."

"No worries. I'm sure Momma has these insured."

"Maybe so, but do *you* want to be the one who tells her that we were careless and lost them?" Jake asked me with a grin.

"Hurry up, would you? I'd like to get these back to her pronto." He'd made a fair point. Momma would understand if something happened to the gems, I just knew it, but I couldn't stand the thought of the disappointment in her face if that happened. The sooner I could turn them back over to her, the better, as far as I was concerned.

"Wow, that smells delicious," I said as Jake and I walked into Momma's cottage that she shared with her husband. The turkey chili she'd had simmering away in the slow cooker all day had filled the house with wondrous smells, and the freshly made biscuits added a nice touch as well.

"It's just chili," my mother said, clearly pleased by my praise. "Phillip, take their coats."

"Yes, dear," he said with a smile. As he took Jake's, he added softly, "There's pie, too."

"I'd be disappointed if there weren't," my husband answered with a grin.

"Now, who's hungry?" Momma asked.

My hand shot up like a third-grader who knew the answer to the teacher's question for the first time in her life. "Me, me."

Jake laughed. "I could eat."

"Excellent," my mother said.

"I didn't answer," Phillip said with a smile.

"Do you really need to?" she asked him with warmth.

"No, not really."

After we sat at the table, Momma served us. The meal at Burt's had been good, but this was better, maybe because it had been made with love, or maybe, just maybe, I'd grown up on this cooking, and every time I tasted it, it felt as though I were going home again.

"Dorothea, you've outdone yourself," Jake said after taking and savoring his first bite.

She smiled at the praise. "I'm so glad you like it."

"That's an understatement," my husband said, and then he turned to me. "Not that I don't love your cooking, too."

"Hey, Momma is the queen. I'd just be honored to be a princess."

"You'll always be my princess," my mother said to me. "Shall we discuss our results or wait until after we eat?"

Jake finished his bite before he spoke. "Let's wait."

"Agreed," Phillip said.

I used my fork to collect a bit of the chili and the pasta mixed into it, and then I tasted my perfect bite. The food might have been plain and ordinary in a less capable cook's hands, but in my mother's, it was magical. I'd tried to duplicate the results at home on my own, and while mine was usually good, hers was amazing. At least I'd gotten her biscuits down pat. "Momma, this is excellent."

"The chili, yes, but you've surpassed the teacher with your biscuits."

"Maybe it's just a donut thing at heart," I said.

After we finished and cleared the table, we all moved into the living room, where a nice fire was waiting for us. We were all so full that we'd decided the pie would have to wait.

"So, who would like to go first?" Momma asked.

"Go on. Why don't you?" Jake urged her.

"We drew some uncooperative folks today, even with the aid of your wondrous donuts, Suzanne. Of the three pawnshops in the area, only one admitted they'd had any contact with loose gemstones at all in the past month."

"Someone tried to sell them in person?" I asked eagerly.

"No, it was a telephone call inquiry."

"Was it a man or a woman?" Jake asked.

"The clerk couldn't tell. Evidently the caller spoke only in a whisper."

"That matches what we learned ourselves," I volunteered. "Whoever took those emeralds from the donut shop is desperately trying to unload them."

"Without success so far, I'd wager," Phillip said.

"I know we ruled it out earlier, but should we be contacting local jewelers as well?" I asked.

Jake shook his head. "No, the prospect of any of them buying stones without a provenance is even more doubtful."

"Then the killer is left dealing with the gray market or even the black one," Momma said.

"Which is harder to access than you might think," Jake said.

"Why is that?"

"Think about it. How would an ordinary citizen even go

about finding someone shady to buy the emeralds from them? Even if they could, would they be able to trust them? I'm not just talking about getting a fair deal, either. What would make them believe that someone willing to buy stolen emeralds wouldn't just take the stones and keep the money or even carry out the transaction and sell the information of who sold them to the insurance company or hand them over to the police?" Jake asked.

"Would a crook actually do that?" I asked.

"He would if he could see a way to profit from it," Phillip answered. "It's been my experience that honor among thieves is merely a myth."

"The insurance company I can understand, but why the police? Explain, please," my mother asked.

"Dorothea, bad guys trade information with law enforcement all the time. If it gets them out of a sticky situation, why wouldn't they? No, I've got a feeling the killer still has those emeralds on them, and they're probably getting edgier and edgier about holding onto them as each hour goes by," Phillip explained.

"So, the real question is how do we use that to our advantage?" I asked.

"That I'm not sure about just yet," Jake said.

Phillip asked, "Did anything else of interest happen on your trip to Maple Hollow?"

"Do you mean besides nearly dying?" I asked him.

"What?" That got my mother's attention. "What happened?"

"Suzanne, there was no way we were in any danger from Lester," Jake said patiently.

"Who's Lester?" Phillip asked.

"It was nothing," Jake explained. "We stopped a brother from bullying his sister. Suzanne's talking about the trip home."

"Okay, I'll bite," Phillip said. "Did someone try to run you off the road or something on your way back here?"

"Nothing quite so dramatic as all that," Jake explained. "We hit a patch of snow on the road, but it turned out fine."

"That's right. I heard it was snowing in Maple Hollow. How bad was it?" Momma asked.

"It was fine," I said, sticking to my husband's nonchalant tone. After all, there was no need to worry Momma after the fact. "Tell them the rest of our findings," I urged Jake.

"It turns out that Deloris has a pretty solid alibi," Jake said. "Besides that, all three of the suspects we have left had a compelling need for money, and fast. Sanderson has a failed business, and the bills are coming due. Madison is overextended on her credit cards and is drowning in debt, while Hank Bloch has an affinity for gambling, even though apparently he's not any good at it."

"Tell them the other thing about Madison," I urged my husband.

"We have reason to believe that she was with a man when we visited her apartment this afternoon," Jake said. "Whether it was Sanderson, Bloch, or someone else entirely, we were unable to determine."

"Forty-eight hours after her boyfriend was murdered?" Phillip asked. "That's kind of cold, isn't it?"

"That describes the woman to a T," I said. "Oh, I forgot to tell you. Deloris came by the shop this morning, though that hardly matters now that she's been cleared, but so did Hank Bloch."

"What did he want?" Momma asked.

"He claimed that he wanted to finish Snappy's last job, and who knows, maybe that really was the only reason he was there, but I had the distinct impression that he was checking the place out."

"Which, as a contractor, he would have naturally done anyway," Jake said.

"True," I said.

"Tell them about the car you saw this morning," Jake prodded me.

"I thought we decided that was nothing."

"Now we need to hear about everything," Momma said.

"Emma and I were outside on our break early this morning when a dark sedan drove by the donut shop. They passed us and turned around, and when I tried to get the plate number, it was obscured by a brown paper bag. It's probably nothing."

"But then Suzanne thought she may have later seen it parked in the apartment complex where Madison lives," Jake added.

"There's no way I can be sure it was the same car, though."

Jake shrugged. "Only time will tell." He paused, and then he smiled at my mother. "Would I be out of line asking about that pie I heard mentioned earlier?"

Momma laughed. "No, I was just thinking the same thing myself. It's apple, with a crisp topping, and I have vanilla ice cream to go with it as well."

"Sold," Jake said with a grin.

"Me, too," I added.

"Make it three," Phillip said.

"Why not an even four?" Momma added with a grin.

By the time Jake and I headed home, it had been dark for a few hours, but there was still one last stop I wanted to make before we got to the cottage.

It was time to check up on the progress at Donut Hearts.

CHAPTER 16

"Wow, it looks incredible, doesn't it," I said as I flipped on the lights at the donut shop and looked around. I knew that the floor had been tiled with long and thin interlocking sections, but it was difficult to tell that the vinyl on the floor wasn't real distressed gray driftwood. The walls had all been covered in real shiplap wood, painted white and antiqued, offering a brightness to the place that hadn't been there before, and the ceiling had been patched beautifully, blending the new seamlessly into the original work perfectly.

Jake whistled under his breath as he took it all in. "This guy is really good."

"How many workers must he have had to do this so quickly?" I asked in awe. The place had literally been transformed in a matter of hours. The only evidence that I could find that the work had been done so recently was the faint smell of paint emanating from the newly installed walls, but he must have used a special paint with low fumes, because it was difficult to detect.

"You'd be surprised. A good crew could do it that fast, and this team is clearly good; there's no doubt about it. What's that?" he asked as he noticed a note sitting on the counter.

"It's from Young," I said as I read it aloud.

"Finished the inside.
Will start on the outside tomorrow.
Door locked and key enclosed.

Young."

"He's a man of few words when he's writing a note, isn't he?" Jake asked me with a grin.

"He can use smoke signals if he wants to, for all I care," I replied. I turned the register on, opened the drawer, and put the key back where it belonged. A part of me felt good having it in my possession again, even though loaning it out had yielded terrific results. "I just wish our case against Snappy's killer was going as smoothly as this remodel is."

"Is it my turn to give you a pep talk?" Jake asked me with a grin. "Keep the faith, Suzanne. We'll get there."

"I hope so."

"Are you ready to go home now, or do you want to stand around and admire the place a little more first?" my husband asked me, still smiling.

"No, we can go. After all, I'll be back here soon enough."

We left the donut shop together, and I felt more at peace than I had before the ice storm had damaged Donut Hearts. I wouldn't be fully recovered until the exterior was repaired as well, but what I'd seen so far had encouraged me.

By this time tomorrow, my shop should be back to its former glory.

There was just one large item still on my checklist that was still nagging me, one that I needed to resolve before I'd be fully able to appreciate all that had happened.

We needed to find Snappy's killer.

The next morning, I was careful not to wake Jake when I left the cottage. Driving through the dark streets of April Springs alone usually gave me a sense of comfort, but this morning I kept seeing demons hiding in the shadows. I parked my Jeep in front of the shop and raced inside, even though I had no real reason to panic. Still, I felt relieved once I was back where I belonged. For the moment, I vowed that things were going to get back to normal as I started the process yet again of making the morning's donuts, but soon enough, it would be time to dig into the murder again. I decided not to focus on that, though, and I found refuge in my work as I made my preparations for a brand-new day. Today happened to be Emma's day off, something she didn't always take every week. I had two days off myself every week when she and her mother, Sharon, took over for me, and I didn't begrudge her the one day she took every now and then herself. The truth of the matter was that I enjoyed working at the donut shop alone, even if it did mean that I'd most likely be buried in dishes until sometime past noon. Alone, the cleaning took on a Zen-like quality, and I found myself getting lost in the process, enjoying the journey as well as the final destination.

That peace was interrupted by my phone ringing two hours before I was set to open for the day.

"Hey, Suzanne. It's Tammy. From Burt's."

"Hi, Tammy. Are you okay?" I asked immediately. "Did Lester decide not to leave town after all?"

"No, he's gone. I watched him get on the bus, and it may be uncharitable to say it, but I hope I never see him again. Your husband is quite a fellow, isn't he?"

"I like to think so. I'm glad you're doing all right."

"I appreciate that. Listen, the reason I'm calling is that I just found out something at the diner, and I knew you'd want to know about it as soon as possible."

"Are you there working already?" I asked as I glanced at the clock. It was just past four, Emma's normal time for coming in if she'd been on the schedule that day.

"I pulled the graveyard shift last night," she said. "I don't mind. We take turns, and my number came up. Nathan Glade came in for a chat and a bite to eat, and he just left."

"I understand. One question."

"What's that?" she wanted to know.

"Should I know that name?" I asked.

Tammy laughed. "That's right. Sometimes I forget you aren't from around here. Nathan is an insomniac who happens to live across the street from Sanderson Mack."

"We've met, actually," I said. "I just didn't know his name. I can't imagine how frustrating it must be for him not to be able to sleep."

"I know. It would drive me crazy, but he likes to come by Burt's and chat with whoever's on duty. The man's the biggest gossip you've ever met in your life, but he's nice enough. Anyway, we got to talking about Snappy and how so many folks had a reason to want to see harm come to him when Nathan said, 'At least his son and his girlfriend are in the clear'."

"What?" I asked. "Why did he say that?"

"Settle down. I'm getting right to it," she said. "Nathan was keeping his usual vigil that night when he saw Madison show up around supper time. He never left his post, and he told me that he saw her roll back out around five a.m., and Sanderson walked her to her car. They thought they were being slick about it, but evidently the two of them have been seeing each other on the side for months."

"Is Nathan sure it was the night before last?" I asked.

"He was dead positive when he told me about it," Tammy said. "I told him to call the police, but knowing Nathan, it's hard to say if he will or not. Anyway, I thought you'd want to know."

"Thank you, Tammy. You may have just provided us with the key to solving this case."

"Hey, I just wanted to do what I could to repay the kindness your husband did for me yesterday," she said softly.

"Well, you can consider that loan paid in full, and then some."

"I'm just glad I could be of help," she said. "Listen, my break is over, so I'd better get back to it."

"I'm sure we'll see you before too long," I said.

"You didn't have to tell me that. I saw the way your husband's eyes lit up when I mentioned the free pie," she answered with a laugh.

I hung up and dialed Chief Grant's number, not even caring that I was probably waking him from a sound sleep.

To my surprise, he sounded downright chipper when he answered my call. "Chief, it's Suzanne. I've got to tell you something about Snappy Mack's murder."

"Suzanne, I can't talk right now," he said in a soft voice. "Are you in any danger?"

"No," I said.

"Then I'll call you back in a bit. Hang tight."

And then he hung up on me.

It wasn't the warmest reception I'd ever received in my life, but then again, I'd gotten worse ones as well.

I decided it was time to call Jake, no matter how late—or early—it might be.

"Jake, Tammy just called me."

"Tell her I can be there in twenty minutes," my husband said, coming fully alert on absolutely no notice at all.

"Hold on. It's not that. She's fine."

"Then why did she call you?"

After I told him what Nathan had conveyed to her about Sanderson and Madison, my husband let out a deep breath. "So, it's Bloch, then."

"That's what I think," I said.

"Have you called the chief to tell him yet?"

"I tried to, but he was in a rush, so he's going to call me back when he gets the chance."

After a long pause, Jake asked, "Suzanne, do you want *me* to follow up with him?"

"No, you go back to bed. I can handle things from here on out."

"Okay, but call me straightaway if you hear anything else, okay?"

"Will do."

Forty-five minutes later, there was a knock on my front door. I peeked outside to find Chief Grant standing there alone with a look of satisfaction on his face.

"Did you catch the killer?" I asked, knowing that it was probably the only thing that could make him grin like that.

"No, but we finally know who did it," he said.

Before he could tell me, I said, "It was Hank Bloch."

The chief looked at me oddly for a moment before he spoke. "How on earth did you know that?"

"I'm right though, aren't I?"

"You are," the chief said, "but I'd still love to know your source."

"It's just the process of elimination," I said. "We know for a fact that Deloris didn't do it; she was with her boyfriend in Tennessee the night of the murder. I just found out from a very credible source that Sanderson Mack and Madison Moore are both innocent. Well, I wouldn't say they were innocent, not by any stretch of the imagination. Let's just say that they aren't guilty of Snappy Mack's murder and leave it at that. The only viable suspect we had left on our list was Hank Bloch, and he certainly had motive enough and the opportunity to do it. How did *you* find out he was the killer?"

"It turned out to be simple police work," the chief said. "Bloch wiped his fingerprints off the screwdriver handle, but he forgot the inside doorknob of your shop. There was no reason for his prints to be there at all, since he's been vehemently denying that he'd ever been in this shop before yesterday. I'm guessing he paid a surprise visit here yesterday, didn't he?"

"Yes. I thought he was here looking for more emeralds," I said.

"Maybe, but what I think is that he was really just covering his tracks. If we hadn't found those prints on the doorknob, we would have never been able to prove that he hadn't left them there when he came to see you yesterday."

"Now that you know who the killer is, what are you doing about it?" I asked him.

"That's where I was when you called me a little while ago. We were getting ready to break into his shop and arrest him. His truck was parked in front, so we thought we had a pretty good idea that he was in there. Only he was gone by the time we got inside."

"So, do you think he's on the run?" I asked.

"Honestly, I'm not even sure he realizes that we know he did it. I'm expecting him back at the shop first thing this morning, acting as though nothing happened. When he shows up, we'll be ready to nab him."

"Good work, Chief," I said, relieved that our independent conclusions had both landed on the same person.

"Right back at you," Chief Grant said with a grin. "Well, I'm off. I'll keep you informed."

"How about some coffee for the road, and maybe a donut or two to go along with it?"

He smiled at me. "You know what? I don't mind if I do. I'll pay my own way, but that sounds great."

"Come on. George won't let me give him any freebies, but he's the mayor. You're a cop. Donuts are your national birthright."

The police chief laughed, but he still shook his head. "As much as I appreciate the offer, I just can't do it."

"Fine, be that way," I said as I stuck my tongue out at him. I took his money, bagged up a few cake donuts I'd just made, and got him a cup of coffee.

Once he was gone, I debated calling Jake when my cell phone rang again.

It was my husband.

"Did you hear the news?" I said. "The Chief agrees with our assessment. He found Hank Bloch's fingerprints on the inside doorknob when he first got here. Thank goodness he and his team were thorough before Bloch could plant his fingerprints other places later."

"So, it's done then. Has he picked him up yet?"

"No, but he believes Hank doesn't even realize his cover is blown. He and Chief Kessler have a team waiting at the construction company's office. The second Hank shows his face, he's going to be under arrest."

"Good. Do you want me to come over and keep you company until we hear for sure that Hank has been arrested?"

"I have a feeling that the last place we need to worry about Hank Bloch showing up is at Donut Hearts. He'll want to avoid this place like the plague now that he believes he's covered his tracks by planting more of his fingerprints around the shop."

"That makes sense, but call me if you need me, okay?"

"I will, but it's not going to happen," I said as I realized that I'd neglected to lock the front door again after the police chief had left. "Good night," I said as I hung up and started toward the front of the shop.

I almost made it, but I wasn't fast enough.

Before I could get the door locked again, Hank Bloch showed up out of the darkness and pushed his way in.

I couldn't even protest.

Having a gun pointed at my heart managed to kill my words before I could speak them.

Evidently I'd made at least one mistake since I'd gotten to the donut shop.

I just hoped that it didn't prove to be a fatal one.

CHAPTER 17

"**Y**OU THINK YOU'RE SO SMART, don't you, Suzanne?" Hank Bloch asked me as he flipped off the main lights at the front of the donut shop. There was still enough light coming from the kitchen to illuminate our surroundings, but no one would be able to see us from outside. "I've been watching you since the start."

"Why are you here?" I asked him in protest. "You should be out of the state by now."

"Don't play stupid with me," he said. "I want the rest of those emeralds before I disappear. I know you found them, so don't try to deny it."

"*Greed*? That's why you came back to the place where you murdered your partner? I don't have them," I said.

"I don't believe you," he said, moving even closer to me with the gun. Bloch was near enough now so that if he pulled the trigger, I knew that I wouldn't stand a chance.

"I'm telling you the truth. I turned them over to the police the moment I found them," I said. I was doing my best to sound convincing, but even though I was mostly telling the truth, my voice still wavered.

Bloch looked disgusted with me, evidently believing me at last. "You're just stupid enough to do exactly that, aren't you? Why didn't you keep them for yourself?"

"Because they never really belonged to me," I said.

"That's why you're running a two-bit donut shop. You don't

have any imagination. This is your building. Of course they belong to you."

"Actually, we haven't been able to figure that out yet," I said.

"Well, you're not getting the ones *I* found," he said, frowning as a car drove by. It was the newspaper delivery guy, but Bloch didn't know that.

"The police are patrolling the neighborhood searching for you. You might as well give yourself up," I said, trying to pull off one of the biggest bluffs of my life.

"Nice try, but no sale," he said, but he still glanced out the window as the car passed by again going in the other direction.

"You didn't realize I'd be out yesterday morning when you drove by the shop, did you? I tried to see who was driving that car, but it was too dark inside to tell. It had to be you, so don't bother trying to deny it."

"Why should I? It was me. I own more than a work truck, Suzanne," he said. "I thought I'd pop over and see if there was anything else of value hidden in your walls here, but evidently you beat me to it."

"The paper bag over the license plate was a nice touch. It really threw me off."

"What can I say? I had to improvise. I can't believe I'm not getting the rest of those emeralds."

"Is that why you killed your business partner? Over a handful of jewels?"

The contractor looked at me with real anger. "I came over here to ask him for a loan, and he laughed at me. He said I could gamble my money away all I wanted to, but I wasn't going to get my hands on any of his. That's when I saw an emerald lying on the floor. I confronted him about it, and the fool tried to hide it from me! He made one last mistake and turned his back on me. The screwdriver was right there, so I used it to shut up his mocking mouth forever."

"You never really dreamed that his will leaving everything to you would stand up in court, did you?" One look at his face told me that I'd just scored a direct hit. "That's why you didn't kill him before," I said. "You couldn't afford to take the chance." I wasn't stalling. I wanted to know the truth. If I was about to die, at least I wouldn't go without knowing what had really happened. "You knew all along that you wouldn't get a dime of his money."

"I would have if he hadn't found out about my little gambling problem. He told me he wasn't about to leave everything he'd worked so hard to acquire to someone who was just going to fritter it all away. As if his son, his girlfriend, or even his ex-wife wouldn't have done the same thing I would have with it."

"Who really gets his money? Do you even know?"

Bloch shrugged. "At this point, it doesn't matter, at least not to me. I guess I'll just have to make do with what I've got. I know one thing. I can't stay here. The police are on to me. I nearly got caught driving home from a poker game this morning, but I happened to see a squad car staking out my house, so I kept driving past."

"Well, you're welcome to my petty cash, but that's all I can give you. If you want to tie me up before you go, there's some duct tape in the back you can use."

Bloch shook his head. "What makes you think I'm going to tie you up?"

"You're going to *kill* me?" I asked, trying to keep the fear out of my voice. "Why? I haven't done a thing to you. No one will find me for hours if you just lock me in the closet in back. You'll be long gone by then."

"Correction. We'll be long gone. You see, you're coming with me."

"What? Why?"

"I need a hostage, just in case," he said, the ice clear in his voice. "If you behave yourself, you might just get through this alive. Now let's go!"

I knew if I left Donut Hearts with this killer, there was a real chance that I'd never live to see the dawn. "What about my money in back? Don't you want that?"

"You said it was petty cash. How much could it be?" he asked me as he glanced back outside again. "Come on. Quit stalling. Nobody's coming to your rescue."

"Do you really think seven emeralds will be enough to last you for the rest of your life?" I asked him.

"It's just five now," Bloch said in disgust.

"What happened to the other two? Did you gamble them away already?"

"In a way, I guess I did just that. I planted the two smallest stones on Sanderson and Madison," he said. "That turned out to be a mistake, but I'll just have to manage as it is. Better to be poor and alive than rich and sitting in jail. Enough stalling. Let's go."

"Can I at least grab my jacket?" I asked. "It's cold out there."

He looked at me suspiciously. "Why, do you have a gun in one of your pockets?"

"No, of course not," I said, wishing that it were true.

"Tough it up. You won't be cold for too long," he said.

That's when I knew that he had never planned on letting me go.

I needed to do something, and it had to be fast, or it was going to be the end of me once and for all.

CHAPTER 18

T HERE WAS A STACK OF folding chairs near the door where Young had left them when he'd left earlier. If I could somehow manage to trip Bloch with them, I might be able to get away from him before he could recover.

As he walked me to the door, I lunged for the chairs, but he was too quick for me, jumping nimbly out of the way before they could even slow him down.

All I'd managed to do was make him even angrier with me.

"Is that the way it's going to be?" I felt the gun barrel being jammed into my back. "Suzanne, do you *want* to die?"

"No, but do I really have any choice?"

"Not if you keep acting like that," he said. "Now go!" Bloch nudged me again, and I had no choice but to cooperate this time.

It was dark outside, with just a dim streetlight down the road offering little illumination. I could see his car, the same black sedan I'd seen the morning before driving past the donut shop, parked off to one side of the parking lot. The contractor moved me quickly to the car, and I decided that I'd have to risk opening the back door as he drove and jumping out, no matter how fast he might be going.

But apparently that wasn't going to happen, either.

Hank Bloch reached for his keys to open the trunk, and I knew that I was going inside.

"I'm afraid of tight spaces," I said, pleading with the man not to stuff me in the trunk. It wasn't entirely true, but I was legitimately terrified that if I got in there, I'd be a dead woman. That part of my fear was real enough.

"It won't be for long. Just until we get out of town."

He started to put his trunk key in the lock when he fumbled it and his key ring slipped to the ground.

I didn't even take a moment to consider my options.

I ran.

There was only one real place I could go. I didn't even consider sticking to the road, even though it would lead me either to Jake or to the police station, depending on the way I chose, but there were streetlights along the way, and I knew that Bloch would be able to pick me off with that gun without a problem. Would he be able to shoot me in the back, though? I didn't want to find out. I tore off across the street and straight into the park. There were trees there, some still down from the ice storm, and it was dark.

If I could get to Jake, maybe he'd be able to save me.

But there was a lot of ground to cover before I made it back to my cottage.

I didn't have to wonder if Bloch would shoot me for very much longer. I heard the gunshot behind me almost at the same time I felt a bullet slam past me, flipping my ponytail before burying itself in a nearby tree.

"Come back here!" Bloch was fully enraged now, shouting at me in the darkness, frustrated by my complete lack of cooperation.

Good.

I didn't waste my breath responding.

As I ran, I kept zigzagging back and forth, doing my best to make myself a hard target to hit. When I risked a glance backward, I saw that he was much too close, running after me with his right arm extended, looking for another clear shot.

Why was he pursuing me and not running away? What good would it do him to kill me now? I wanted to shout out his illogical behavior, but I needed every gasp of breath I had just to stay alive.

Another shot rang out, and it felt even closer than the last one had. I braced myself for impact, but it never came.

Dodging behind a tree for some cover, my foot hit an exposed root, and I felt myself going down. I tried to scramble back onto my feet, but I must have twisted my ankle during the fall!

I was dead, and I knew it.

As Bloch came toward me, he slowed a little, smiling in the dim light at my predicament.

But I wasn't finished yet.

I frantically felt around on the ground for something, anything I could use in my own defense. My hands closed on some dried leaves and a bit of a branch that had fallen during the ice storm. As Bloch approached, I did my best to fling the leaves directly in his face, and then I quickly followed up by swinging the branch toward his gun, hoping to dislodge it and buy myself some time.

Both of my attempts failed miserably, but at least I'd tried.

There was nothing else to do but face my fate.

That wasn't entirely true, though.

With what very well might have been my final breath, I screamed out my husband's name. "Jake!" It might be the last thing I ever said in this world, but if that was how my life was to end, I wanted to die with my husband's name on my lips.

"Drop it," I heard my dear, sweet spouse's voice say from the darkness a split second later.

Bloch started to swing his pistol around to the sound of Jake's voice as well.

"Last chance," Jake said coldly, and I could hear the Angel of Death in his voice.

Evidently so could the contractor.

Hank Bloch dropped the weapon instantly, and once more, perhaps for the final time, I was miraculously saved at the last possible second.

CHAPTER 19

T HREE DAYS LATER, MY ANKLE fine again, I was back at the donut shop serving my customers their donuts for the day when Jake walked in.

"That's not a happy look on your face," I said the moment I saw his frown.

"It's fine. It's just that nobody's sure what happened to the five emeralds Bloch supposedly had on him when the Chief searched him after his arrest. It's as though they just vanished into thin air."

"He couldn't have swallowed them, could he?"

"No, they would have turned up by now if that were the case," Jake said as he shook his head.

"Have they still not found the gems he planted on Sanderson and Madison?" I asked as I got him a cup of coffee.

"They haven't turned up either, and the pair won't admit to finding them on their own. My best guess is that they discovered the emeralds and decided to keep them for themselves. It would be just like them, wouldn't it?"

"They're like a pair of dogs fighting over table scraps," I said, wondering how that unholy alliance would ever last.

"Have you heard any word on who is going to eventually get Snappy's money?" Jake asked me.

"As a matter of fact, Adam just called," I said. "Evidently, Snappy had a change of heart in the end and gave it all to Deloris after all. There was a will that he'd had notarized two days before he died and a note attached to it. He explained that the failure of their marriage was mostly his fault, and if he had it all to do over again, he never would have left her. It was his way of apologizing for being such a miserable husband. Actually, it was kind of sweet the way it all worked out in the end."

"So, Sanderson and Madison are going to have to make do with the illicit gains from the sale of two small emeralds. I wish there was a way to keep them from even getting that much," Jake said. "Snappy might have been a decent businessman, but he certainly surrounded himself with some less-than-stellar people, including his own son."

"It's not much of a legacy to leave behind, is it?" I asked.

"No, it's not," Jake agreed. He finally smiled as he looked at me. "The outside looks just as good as the inside, doesn't it?"

"I'd hire Young again in a heartbeat. He and his crew do excellent work."

"Let's hope you never need him," Jake said. "Have you thought any more about the emeralds you found here?"

"According to Momma's lawyer, their fate will be tied up in court for years. There are so many claims on them they may never sort it out. The insurance company wants them, four surviving Hathaway heirs are filing counterclaims, and Momma is urging me to put my two cents in as well."

"What are you going to do?" Jake asked me.

"On the face of it, I'd feel foolish not to at least try, don't you think? Especially with Momma offering to foot the legal expenses, something we surely can't afford on our own."

"How do you feel about her doing that?" Jake asked me.

"If it's okay with you, I say we take her up on her kind offer. Momma's not doing it for free, though. She's offering me a fifty-fifty split if we win. If you ask me, I think she's doing it for the sheer fun of it."

Jake laughed. "That sounds good to me. Why not roll the dice and see what happens?"

"Be careful there. That's what got Hank Bloch in trouble in the first place," I reminded him.

"I thought his game of choice was poker," Jake said.

"You well know what I mean. So, would you like a donut to go with that coffee?"

I was expecting him to turn me down, but instead, he grinned and said, "I wouldn't mind an old-fashioned cake donut at that."

"You're such a risk taker," I said as I got him his usual fare.

"Tell you what. Make it iced," Jake said.

"Wow, now you're really living on the edge."

"What can I say? We need to grab life and get the most out of it that we can."

"I couldn't agree with you more," I said as I got him his donut.

On impulse, I grabbed one for myself, and since we were slow at the moment, I carried both treats around the counter, and we sat at one of the new pieces of furniture my friends had given me after the ice storm. As we ate and chatted, I looked around the donut shop. The shiplap whitewashed walls were perfect, and the patterned gray wood simulated hardwood floors looked as though they'd been there for a hundred years.

I promised myself that I wouldn't be upset about the court's decision as to who the emeralds eventually belonged to, no matter what they ended up deciding.

After all, I was already the richest woman in town if the love and affection of my husband, my family, my friends, and my customers counted for anything.

And for me, they meant everything!

RECIPES

Momma's Turkey Chili (NEW)

We used to make a variation of this recipe with ground beef, but lately we've switched to ground turkey or even chicken. I've served this to guests who've had no idea it wasn't my regular ground beef chili, and it's fast become a favorite of mine. The heat of the chili can be adjusted accordingly, but I strongly suggest including at least a little chili powder for the flavor range it brings. My spouse suggested the pasta addition long ago after attending the University of Kentucky, which happens to be close to Ohio, and this is a variation of the famed Cincinnati Chili. With or without the pasta, though, this recipe is a real keeper!

Ingredients

- 1 pound ground turkey (ground chicken or ground beef 80/20 can be substituted)
- 1 medium onion, diced, yellow or white
- 1 medium green bell pepper, diced
- 1 medium red (or yellow) bell pepper, diced
- 1 15-oz. (approximate) can tomato sauce
- 1 to 3 tablespoons chili powder (depending on the amount of heat you like)
- 1 teaspoon sugar
- 1 teaspoon salt

- 1 teaspoon black pepper
- 1 teaspoon Worcestershire sauce
- * Approximately 1 tablespoon olive oil needed to cover the bottom of the pan if poultry is used
- 1 15-oz. (approximate) can dark-red kidney beans, drained
- 2 to 4 oz. cooked spaghetti noodles, added just before serving (amount is matter of preference)

Directions

In a large pan, brown the ground meat, diced onion, and diced green and red bell peppers until thoroughly cooked. Add the tomato sauce, chili powder, sugar, salt, pepper, and Worcestershire sauce and stir in thoroughly, then bring to a boil. Back off the heat to a simmer, cover, and cook for one hour, stirring occasionally. Add the drained kidney beans, stir them in, and then heat throughout for 15 to 20 minutes. Just before serving, add the pasta, incorporating it thoroughly before dishing it out.

Feeds 3 to 4 people.

Lemon Donut Treats

There's something about the taste of lemon to me, whether in a donut, a drink, a pie, or a bowl of sherbet. My family has learned to indulge me when I go through these periods of lemon craziness, mostly because they're just as passionate about my lemon donuts as I am. To add a little more zest to the treats, I've formulated a simple lemon glaze that enhances the donuts into pure delight!

Ingredients

Mixed
- 1 egg, lightly beaten
- 1/2 cup whole milk (2% will do)
- 1 tablespoon canola oil (any vegetable oil will do)
- 1 1/2 teaspoons lemon extract

Sifted
- 1 cup flour, unbleached all-purpose
- 1/2 cup sugar, granulated
- 1 teaspoon baking soda
- 1/4 teaspoon nutmeg
- 1/4 teaspoon cinnamon
- 1/4 teaspoon salt

Directions

Preheat your oven to 365 degrees F.

In a large bowl, beat the egg lightly, and then add the milk, canola oil, and lemon extract. Set this aside, and in another medium-sized bowl, sift together the flour, sugar, baking soda, nutmeg, cinnamon, and salt.

Slowly add the dry ingredients to the wet, stirring along the way until the mix has a smooth consistency.

Place the batter in a greased donut pan and bake for seven to nine minutes or until the donuts are a golden brown but not too dark.

Remove the donuts to a cooling rack, and while they are still warm, drizzle them with the lemon glaze mentioned below for a truly delightful treat!

Yield: 8 to 10 small donuts

Lemon Glaze

This is a simple and easy glaze that's sure to be a hit! We like it not only on our lemon donuts but on pound cake, sugar cookies, and anything else we can think of! For a little added zip, add the zest of half a lemon to the mixture as well.

- 1/2 cup confectioner's sugar
- 1 tablespoon warm water
- 1/2 teaspoon lemon extract
- (The zest from half a lemon, optional)

In a medium-sized bowl, mix confectioner's sugar, water, and lemon extract. Combine until the sugar is dissolved into a glaze and then drizzle on top of the donuts while they are still warm.

My Favorite Apple Pie Recipe

There are times when I love a good double-crust apple pie, but lately the only pie my family clamors for is one with a crisp topping. We've even made this without the crust on occasion, but for my taste, it's best when it's served as pie. I was going to say plain and simple, but there's nothing plain *or* simple about this recipe. Add a scoop of vanilla bean ice cream to the top of a warm piece of pie, and it's just about as close to perfection in the kitchen as you're ever going to get! This pie is wonderful fresh out of the oven and piping hot or served a day or two later, either served at room temperature or straight from the refrigerator, though most of my pies never make it that long!

Ingredients

- 5–6 cups thinly sliced firm, tart apples
- (Granny Smiths work well in this recipe, as do Staymen and Gala. I like to mix my apples, using three-quarters Granny Smith and one-quarter Staymen or Gala)
- 1/2 cup granulated sugar
- 3 tablespoons all-purpose unbleached flour
- 1 teaspoon nutmeg
- 1 teaspoon cinnamon
- Dash of salt
- 8 – or 9-inch pie crust (premade is fine, or make your own if you're so inclined)
- Topping
- 1 cup all-purpose unbleached flour
- 1/2 cup brown sugar
- 1/2 cup butter, room temperature

Directions

Peel and core the apples, then cut them into thin slices, mixing them all together well in the bowl afterward to get a good blend of your varieties. In a medium bowl, sift together the sugar, flour, nutmeg, cinnamon, and salt, then stir into the apples until they are thoroughly coated. Add the coated apple slices to the pie shell and set it aside.

In another medium-sized bowl, combine the flour and brown sugar, and then cut in the chilled butter. The mix should be crumbly, and the butter will be in small pieces around the size of a BB. Add the topping to the pie, and then bake it uncovered in a 425-degree-F oven for 30 to 45 minutes until the crust is golden brown and delicious. Check the top frequently for scorching, and when it gets to be a dark brown, cover it loosely with foil and continue to bake until a butter knife slips into the top easily. Cool at least 10 minutes if you can wait, and then add a scoop of ice cream before serving if you are so inclined.

Serves 4 to 8 (4 if you're being generous, 8 if you're feeling stingy) depending on your slices and the level of your hunger!

If you enjoy Jessica Beck Mysteries and you would like to be notified when the next book is being released, please send your email address to **newreleases@jessicabeckmysteries.net**. Your email address will not be shared, sold, bartered, traded, broadcast, or disclosed in any way. There will be no spam from us, just a friendly reminder when the latest book is being released.

Also, be sure to visit our website at jessicabeckmysteries.net for valuable information about Jessica's books.

OTHER BOOKS BY JESSICA BECK

The Ghost Cat Cozy Mysteries
Ghost Cat: Midnight Paws
Ghost Cat 2: Bid for Midnight

The Cast Iron Cooking Mysteries
Cast Iron Will
Cast Iron Conviction
Cast Iron Cover Up
Cast Iron Motive
Cast Iron Suspicion

60313209R00099

Made in the USA
Lexington, KY
03 February 2017